Dragon:

Our Tales

RAGON:
Our Tales

Vol.4 of Indian Creek Anthology Series

© 2014 Southern Indiana Writers

The Southern Indiana Writer's Group

Dragon: Our Tales
Volume 4 of the Indian Creek Anthology Series

Third Edition

Published by Southern Indiana Writers, 2200 Reno Ave., New Albany, IN, 47150
Book designed by T. Lee Harris

ISSN 1085-357X
ISBN 978-0-9882664-7-6

Cover Art and design by T. Lee Harris Based on a design by Marian Allen

First Edition 1997
Second Edition 2007
Third Edition 2014

Dragon:
Our Tales

Contents

1 Blossom on the Water .... Marian Allen

5 Illustration .... Joy Kirchgessner

21 The Slaying of the Dragon .... Jeannine Baumgartle

22 Illustration .... Joy Kirchgessner

28 The Dragon Within .... Glenda Mills

29 Buenos Noches .... Marla Bilbrey

33 Illustration .... Joy Kirchgessner

38 Nede .... Jeannine Baumgartle

40 Sometimes Da Dragon Wins.................................... Ginny Fleming

41 Illustration .... Joy Kirchgessner

52 Six Lies of the Dragon .... Marla Bilbrey

54 Slaying Summer's Dragon .... Dirk D. Griffin

75 Illustration .... Joy Kirchgessner

76 Dragon's Tears .... Ginny Fleming

77 The Dragon Incident .... Elizabeth J. Gross

85 Illustration .... Joy Kirchgessner

88 Sanctum Ad Terminus .... Jeannine Baumgartle

89 The Jade Dragon .... T. Lee Harris

90 Illustration .... T. Lee Harris

99 The Transformation .... Marian Allen

101 The Hired Hand .... Joy Kirchgessner

106 Illustration .... Joy Kirchgessner

110 Dragon's Lair .... Glenda Mills

114 Illustration .... Joy Kirchgessner

118 Contributors

121 Also by Southern Indiana Writers

Blossom On the Water
Marian Allen

I've known Bud from the cradle up — my cradle, that is; Bud's been around since long before my time. Everybody knew Bud — only Chinese guy in a town the size of Shepherds, Indiana, everybody's bound to know him. Had the best restaurant in town, too, though I guess that's not saying much.

Bud wasn't really Chinese, of course. I mean, he looked Chinese, but he was an American — at least, we all guessed he was: He dressed like an American, and he talked like an American, and you know what they say about ducks. His name was Bud Blossom, and us kids thought that was pretty funny.

He said his real name was Chinese, but it meant something like "bud" and "blossom" and if you laughed he'd tell you what your name meant. That was okay if it was, like, "manly" or even "ruler of the home," but if it was "bald" or "pea field" — well, we got to where we left him alone about his name.

I asked my Dad once how long Bud had been around, and Dad said, "He come down here from New York in 1957. They said he walked into the bank with a wad of cash on him that would choke a mule. Never said where he got it. We always figured he stole it. Thought somebody might come after him for it, but they never did, so we stopped thinking it. He opened that place of his on Cherokee Creek, and he's been here ever since."

Cherokee Creek ran right through town — if you can

call 5,000 people a town. The "creek" was nearly a river, a tributary of the Ohio; it was too wide to jump and too deep to wade, especially above the reservoir east of town. Bud's restaurant was on a houseboat up at the docks, with some tables inside and some tables outside under a red-and-yellow striped canopy.

It was named The Golden Lotus, but everybody called it Bud's. My Mom and Dad had their first date there. After I was born, they took me with them. It was that kind of a place — a little bit ratty, so it didn't matter if your kids chewed on the booth backs. Sold chop suey, chow mein, fried rice, egg rolls, fried chicken, steak, slaw, fish, baked potatoes, and hamburgers.

Lots of times I would walk up there after school if nobody was going to be home and kill some time with Bud. He'd work me while we talked, but I didn't mind working for Bud. Sometimes we'd fish, dropping lines over the side of the restaurant.

"Freshest fish possible," he would say at least once while we were reeling them in. "Caught off the side of the boat they're served in. Can't get fish fresher than that."

"That'd be true, if you served 'em now, but we're going to clean 'em and freeze 'em. Might as well have 'em flown in from China or Mexico."

He never would admit to that — always claimed his fish was fresh caught. That was Bud.

***

When I hit fourteen, I went to work for him for pay. Bud and Mom and Dad and I filled out a bunch of papers and signed a bunch of stuff; I could only work so many hours and not during school hours or after such-and-such

o'clock and all that. I helped clean and cook and fish and carried orders out to the dock . . . all the stuff that I'd have done for nothing anyway — had been doing for nothing, anyway. Saturdays, I slept over and worked past closing, helping him get set up for the Sunday after-church rush. We didn't report that as time on the job, and he gave me a "gift" every week equal to what I'd be making if I'd been "working."

That's when I found out Bud drank. I don't know if the grown-ups knew about it or not; nobody ever said anything about it to me, and I never said anything about it to anybody else. Plum wine, is what he drank. He sold it from behind the register, along with little silk dolls with paper parasols, and cellophane-wrapped boxes of "Chinese Restaurant Tea," and colored plastic toothpicks shaped like swords. He'd drive off in his red Mazda and come back with two crates of wine in the trunk and I'd help him in with it. The labels were purple and olive, pictures of plums, with gold Chinese writing on them. Beautiful labels, and the glass of the bottles was transparent green.

So this Saturday night after the first time I helped him unload the wine, he got out five bottles and started through them. I never saw a man drink like that — he drank like he was paying taxes or marching in the mud. Sour look on his face.

"Kenny," he said at last. "I hope you never know what it's like to be away from home and no way back."

"You and me both," I said. "I don't even want to go in the army. See the world? What for?"

"Exactly." Bud nodded and shook a finger, like his head

and his hand were both agreeing with me. "What for?"

It made me feel kind of sad and jealous, but I said, "You wish you were back in New York?"

"New York? . . .No."

We both went back to work; me sweeping and him drinking.

After a while, he said, "In China, this river would have a god."

"The Ohio?"

"Yes, the Ohio, but I mean this . . . this . . . this creek. Cherokee Creek would have a god, a king, a lord. Not a man, you understand? A king under the water."

"A Kingfish?" I started laughing. Kingfish is a restaurant in Louisville, and I thought he was joking.

"A dragon," he said, his voice so calm he had to be trying hard to make it that way. I looked at him, then: His eyes were narrow slits, his nostrils were flared, and the corners of his mouth were drawn down tight. I could see his teeth glinting from between his lips and I'll tell you I was a little bit scared.

"No offense," I said, holding on to the broom and standing real still. This was my first run-in with a binge drunk and I didn't know what to do or say. "I didn't understand at first. There'd be a dragon in Cherokee Creek, if it was in China?"

Bud relaxed some, and so did I — some.

"More important than that," he said, "everyone would believe there was a dragon — even those who 'knew better.' He would have a name, and a personality and qualities, just like another townsperson, except he would be honored and sacrificed to."

"No offense," I said, holding on to the broom and standing real still.

"Sacrificed? Like . . . how?" The Aztecs had made a bad impression on me, and the word sacrifice called up very unpleasant associations.

"Rice cakes and paper flowers and foil fish with ribbons for tails. . . . Clay figures, music. . . ."

"You've been to China? You sound like you've seen it."

"Yes. Yes, I've seen it." Bud opened another bottle and poured.

"Is that where you want to go back to, but you can't?"

I don't know if he didn't hear me, or heard me wrong, or decided to ignore me, or thought he was answering, but he said:

"Once or twice a century, the water lord would select a bride from the local population. Her family would dress her up in the finest cloth and richest jewels the town could provide, and everybody would row out into the river or the lake, and there would be music. The people would throw gifts into the water and the girl would jump overboard to meet her bridegroom."

"She would, huh?" I wasn't able to keep flat disbelief out of my voice.

Bud snickered. "Sometimes she had to be helped over the side. Her clothes would become heavy with water, and she would sink. Then her bridegroom would claim her and take her to his palace. Sometimes she would live happily for the rest of her life with the faithful love of an immortal. Sometimes . . . she wasn't so lucky."

"They must have a lot of pretty girls in China, to drown them like that." Sounded worse than the Aztecs to me, but I didn't say that. I doubted any of it was true, anyway. I mean, certainly not the happy palace part, but

probably not any of it.

"A lot of pretty girls," Bud said.

"Were you ever married?" I asked suddenly.

Bud looked up, one hand around his glass and one around the bottle. "Why?"

"No reason. Just asked."

He nodded.

"She lived with me in my family's home. I was not a good husband to her. She killed herself. My family threw me out. And here I am."

He started to cry: big, round drops fell one after the other onto the table, but he didn't blubber or try to talk anymore. I finished sweeping and went to bed.

＊＊＊

Bud didn't drink like that every Saturday: Just the days he brought the wine. Then he'd get those five bottles and start in. I'd get the sweeping done as soon as I could and go to my cabin; I didn't want to hear any more of Bud's history — personal or cultural.

I couldn't forget it, though. Mom would watch a Public Television show about China, or we'd get a multi-cultural textbook in History, and I'd see it again the way Bud had described it to me: The boats, the Fourth-of-July atmosphere, the rice cakes and flowers, the young girl drowning while everyone cheered.

＊＊＊

I had my first date in Junior High. Bud started giving me advice then, and kept giving it on through High School, although I never asked him for it. I'm glad to say I never took it, either — I mean, who in his right mind would take

interpersonal relationship tips from a guy who thought drowning a girl was an excuse for a party?

For instance:

"Why don't you ask that Fentress girl to the movies?"

"She's going with Todd Martin."

"What does that have to do with it?"

". . .Because she'd say no, for one thing."

Bud grinned. "Maybe. Maybe not. You don't know until you try. Tell her I gave you a two-for-one dinner ticket and she's the one you want to share it with. Here, I'll give you one."

"No, Bud. Thanks, but. . . . Why would I want to go out with a girl who'd run around on her boyfriend? If she'd two-time him, why wouldn't she two-time me?"

He shrugged. "Who cares? It's just a date. She's pretty. You'd have a good time."

And I got to thinking, He's right. It's just a high school date. She's just a pretty girl. I'd have a good time, and she's the one who'd have to face Todd, because I could knock his brains out and he knows it.

And then I started planning how I'd talk her into it, and then I heard in my head what the other guys — and the girls — would say about me if I did it, and my Mom and Dad. What I'd think of me if I did it. One good time — even at half-price — just wasn't worth it.

But Bud was telling me that it would have been worth it to him, and I'd get that freaky feeling again, that feeling I had the first night I saw him drinking: the feeling that Bud maybe wasn't the simple, decent neighborhood business-man we all thought he was.

✳✳✳

I decided to go to a community college, not far from Shepherds. I lived on-campus, but came home most week-ends, at least for the first year.

I worked at Bud's that summer. He treated me more like an adult than he had before I went away. The funny thing — well, the odd thing — was that treating me like an adult meant that there was a wall between us that had never been there before. It was like he had this mask he wore for all the grown-ups and, now that I was getting to be a grown-up, I got the mask treatment just like all the others. I resented the hell out of it.

※

The first week of my sophomore year, I fell in love with Meredith DeLint from my History of Science class, and she turned out to be from just over the county line, and she came home with me to meet Mom and Dad, and we took her to Bud's for dinner.

And Bud fell in love with her, too.

Meredith was a beauty: Straight black hair she kept cut shoulder-length, clear pink skin, dark eyes, petite but . . . you know . . . built.

I was used to guys looking at her like they wished she had come in alone, but when I saw that same look on Bud's face. . . . It made me sick. It was almost as if I'd seen it on Dad.

He came over and greeted us, which he almost never does, and took Meredith's elbow and led her to a table, smiling and moving close to murmur in her ear, as if he didn't want to shout over the other customers' voices.

When he seated us, he flashed me his teeth like . . .

not like a challenge, because we both knew he didn't see it as a contest. It was like he was saying, You know what I'm going to do. Do you really think you can stop it?

I looked him over: about 5'6", slim, looking like a wimp but, I knew from seeing him with his shirt off, tightly muscled; flat black hair and bright black eyes, skin a dark gold, perfect teeth. Deep creases at the corners of his eyes and mouth, but girls go for a "face with character" sometimes. I took Meredith's hand.

"No PDA's." Dad growled it so I'd know it was half a joke.

He meant Public Displays of Affection. Forbidden on school property. It was in the manuals and everything.

"This isn't a PDA," Meredith said. "This is first aid. His hands are like ice."

I don't think they warmed up all evening. Bud didn't hover or do anything obvious. Mom and Dad would have commented if he'd been too obvious — everybody in the restaurant would have. It's a very small town; we know one another's surfaces like we know the fronts of the stores on Broad Street. But I knew Bud below the surface — far enough below it, anyway, to see him turning something on I'd never seen him use before. And I could see Meredith responding, unaware.

We had a fight about it while I drove her home.

"Okay, maybe he was flirting with me a little bit. I didn't see it but, as you say, you know him better than I do. What if he was?"

"You were flirting back!"

"I was not! Or, if I was, it was innocent. You know, like when your Dad said he wished he'd seen me first and I batted my eyes at him. . . ."

"Dad didn't mean it."

"I've never seen you like this! You've never been jealous before, why should you be so silly now? And over him, of all people."

That was like a stone hitting my heart. I mean, the way she said him instead of "Bud." Like there was only one "him" she could possibly be talking about.

I didn't take her to Bud's again, but she went on her own. A buddy told me, one Monday, he'd seen her there over the weekend when she'd gone home and I hadn't.

"How's Bud?" I asked, when I saw her again.

"Fine," she said, and flipped her hair the way girls do to show they're being casual about something. "He said to give you his love."

"Tell him hello from me, the next time you see him," I said, knowing she'd see him again, heavy with knowing I couldn't keep her from it.

"You aren't still jealous, are you?"

I looked her dead in the eye and said, "I trust you." It's my old friend, Bud, I don't trust. But I didn't say that.

✳✳✳

It sort of broke us up, her seeing Bud. She wouldn't stop it, no matter what I said. She claimed she had a right to have her own friends. She asked what was I jealous of: my relationship with her or my friendship with Bud? It got to be a kind of control/freedom conflict and we finally stopped seeing each other.

I worked for Bud again that summer, although it was like fooling with a loose tooth:

Every morning, Bud would ask, "Heard from Meredith?"

If I said, "No," he'd tell me about the last time he'd

called her — or she'd called him. If I said, "Yes," he'd ask what she had to say and laugh and slap me on the back if I wouldn't repeat our conversation.

At least he didn't try to talk about her, like the guys in the locker room used to compare notes on girls in High School. I wouldn't have tolerated that, which was probably the only thing that stopped him — he knew me so well, he could judge to an inch how far he could push me.

And, whether I got used to Meredith's having a life outside of the time she shared with me, or whether I grew up, or what, I started our Junior year by apologizing to her. The next time I took her to Bud's, during Spring Break, Meredith and I were engaged, planning a three-year engagement and a summer wedding.

❋

It was the end of May our Junior year, and school was just out. The weather had turned off warm, and Meredith was supposed to meet me at my house. She and Mom and Dad and I were going on an afternoon picnic; the first picnic of the year.

The doorbell rang. I answered the door. It was Frank Ossterman, one of the three state troopers stationed in town, my supervisor on the Volunteer Disaster Response Team.

Frank just stood there after I said "Hello," holding his hat by the brim with one hand and playing with the hat-band's tassels. His eyes flickered up to meet mine, then flicked away.

"The water's up over the road a couple of places on Cherokee Ridge," Frank said.

"Little late to sandbag, then," I said. "Are we evacuating people? Want me to get Dad?"

"No, no, the creek's crested. . . ." Frank shifted on his feet and sighed as if he'd accepted a heavy burden and might as well get on with it.

"She wasn't going too fast," he said, "but she hit one of those spots and hydroplaned. Car went out of control and went into the creek there at the reservoir. A couple of guys fishing saw it happen. She was washed out of the car and over the dam."

"Oh, my God!" I felt behind me for my jacket on the hall rack. "Are they sure the car's empty? We better check. She might have had a kid strapped in—"

Frank stared at me, startled, then his face went pale. "I'm talking about Meredith," he said. "God, I'm sorry to have to tell you."

They hadn't found a body yet but, if they found anything, it would be a body and not my Meredith. The fishermen had seen her swept away, face down. My Meredith.

Frank told Mom and Dad. I must have walked into the living room and sat down, because that's where I was when I looked up and saw Dad blotting his tears on the sleeve of his flannel shirt. Mom sat on the couch, rocking back and forth and sobbing softly into a tissue. Frank was gone. The sun was low.

I stood up, still dry-eyed.

"I'm going for a walk. I gotta get some fresh air."

The Super-Mart was three miles away and I turned toward it. There was a jumble in my head, a rummage of mixed-up thoughts, tied together with a sense that I needed to get something; that if I got it, everything would be all right.

Part of the rummage was Bud's old story of the drowned bride. Sacrifices to the King Under the Water. Bud, letting me know that a pretty girl was a good time, even if she was my love.

I stopped at the Bottle Bin and made a few selections. Down the road out of sight, I opened one and knocked about a third of it back. I dropped the empty bottle in a trash can just inside the Super-Mart.

❋

By the time I got to Bud's, it was past midnight. The restaurant was dark, just the floods on the dock lighting the deck. I managed to get aboard without falling off the gangplank and used my key to let myself in.

I knew Bud had to have heard me. He must have known it was me; after all these years, he had to know my feet. He didn't come out into the restaurant, though. Maybe he thought I'd go away.

I called him, finally.

"Bud! C'mon out here, 'my friend.' Let's talk!"

He came out of his cabin, smoothing his hair. He was wearing red cotton pajamas. No slippers.

"I heard about Meredith," he said. "I'm sorry. . . ."

Then he saw the table, covered with my purchases. A bottle of Indiana wine (the last of three), a man's gold ring with diamond chips, a windsock shaped like a long-tailed fish, a bottle of local wild honey, and a package of those Quaker Puffed Rice things that people on diets eat — the only kind of rice cakes we get in Southern Indiana.

"Is this enough?" I said. "You want more? Just tell me, and I'll get it. Anything. Anything. Just give her back. Please, give her back."

I had never seen Bud look stunned before. He shook his head slowly, eyes on the table of gifts.

"I don't have her. She's gone. She drowned, Kenny. Kenny, I want you to know this: Meredith was true to you. She never took so much as a free dessert from me, and she never gave me more than a smile."

"You want 'em in the water?" I shouted, feeling my face heat up with the power of tears unshed. "You got 'em in the water!"

I gathered up the corners of the blue linen tablecloth and carried the bundle outside. I swung it, released two corners, and watched my sacrifices fly out of the floodlight, listened to them splash. I carried the tablecloth back in and smoothed it over the table.

"Now," I said.

"Kenny. . . ." Bud held out empty hands. "I don't have her. She drowned."

"Just a girl, right?" I said. My legs stopped supporting me then, and my head forgot which way was up. "She was just another pretty girl?"

***

I woke with a pounding headache. I was in my own bed, and Mom was bending over me with a couple of pills and a glass of water.

Dad stood behind her. "Had you a snootful, huh? Boy, you are way too big for me to still be carrying you home from Bud's!"

Bud's. I had been to Bud's and made a fool of myself. I'd have to go apologize. . . . Sometime. . . .

"Honey," Mom said, "Frank was by earlier."

I took the pills and drank the water. My hand was

trembling.

Mom looked at Dad. He nodded to her and she said, "They found her. Meredith. Alive. They don't know how it happened, but she survived."

"She's pretty beat up from the rocks and stuff," Dad said. "Broke a collarbone. They had to pump out her stomach and clear her lungs, but she's fine. No brain damage or anything. She's just fine. She's in the county hospital." Dad leaned over Mom and patted my shoulder. "She'll be ready to see you by the time you clean up and get over there."

That's when I started to cry. Mom held me and Dad left the room and I cried myself out.

When I had finished, Mom said, "There's something else. . . ."

I swung my legs out of bed and thought about what to wear for Meredith's return from the dead.

"Honey, there's something else."

"What?"

"It's Bud. He's in the hospital, too."

"Bud. . . ?"

"Frank found him this morning. He was on the dock, like he was trying to get back to the restaurant. He was in his pajamas. Barefoot. He'd been . . . been mugged, I guess. They . . . they hurt him."

"Hurt him how?"

"They . . . cut his eye. They cut it out."

***

I drove myself to the hospital and stood in the lobby, unable to decide on who to ask for first — the woman I loved, or the man whose friendship I'd denied and reviled

— until Holly, the receptionist, said,

"Meredith's in 230, hon."

Meredith never looked so beautiful, but she was so pale — as if she'd been years out of the sun. She remembered going into the water, and she remembered feeling the sandbank under her hands, and that was all until she came around in the hospital. When I left her room, we had moved our wedding plans up to right after graduation. We'd have had the hospital chaplain perform the service right then and there, but we had some sense left, I guess.

Then Bud. I felt guilty, as if my senseless fury had been a beacon to draw violence down on him.

He lay in the hospital bed, his head half-covered in bandages. Frank was with him.

"If you think of anything else, let us know," Frank said to him. "But this isn't much to go on. I don't think we're going to nail these guys, I gotta tell you."

"I know," Bud said. "They make it their business not to be nailed. They're very good at it. At least I don't have to worry about it happening any more."

Frank turned to me. "Great news about Meredith! Wish I could have been the one to tell you." He slapped me on the back and left.

I walked closer until I stood at the foot of the bed.

"Bud. . . . I can't believe how stupid I was last night."

He waved a hand. "You weren't the only one who was stupid last night. Sit down."

I moved one of the chairs to where he could see me and sat.

Bud adjusted his pillow so it didn't obstruct his view and said, "I can't believe you remembered that story I told about the Dragon Festival . . . about the gifts, the sacrifices."

I shifted in my chair, unable to extract the right words from all the ones I could have used.

"Let me tell you another story from the old country," Bud said:

"There was a mighty dragon king, as noble as he was powerful. This king had a brother, weak and selfish. The brother was always making mischief — not the innocent kind we mean over here, but the dangerous, hurtful kind. Once, he saw a woman on the bank of the lake. He fancied the woman, and he stole her. The woman begged to be released, but the wicked brother wouldn't, and no one could interfere between a dragon and his wife, not even the dragon king. One day, the woman snatched a jeweled dagger from a pile of treasure and killed herself. At that, the dragon king cursed his evil brother and banished him from his court forever."

Bud stopped and licked his lips. I handed him his water glass. He sipped, his one eye fixed on me, handed back the glass, and went on.

"The wicked brother never changed his ways. He didn't indulge his nature much in exile, because opportunities were so limited, but his spirit was unaltered. Then an opportunity arose and the wicked brother seized it. Tried to seize it. But the maiden he tried to steal proved stronger than he had expected and, before he could overcome her strength, she died. She died a natural death by drowning."

We looked at each other, neither of us moving, then Bud turned his head to stare at the ceiling.

"That's when the wicked brother found that he had

been corrupted by his years away from his own kind. His grandeur had been eroded. His wickedness, once as tremendous as his great brother's nobility, was no longer a perfect sphere, but was full of pits and holes. He found that out when he saw how the girl's death hurt someone else and, more important, when he saw that he cared about that hurt."

Bud sighed. "So, the wicked brother returned to the dragon king and begged him to use his influence with the Great King of Heaven to return the girl to life. The dragon king agreed. But, there would be a price. The wicked brother would have to give his eye in payment for the girl. His right eye."

Bud's hand went to the bandage on his face, touching the place the muggers had destroyed.

"And, because the wicked brother had finally managed to do a good deed, he was offered a second chance. His exile was revoked; if his improvement seemed permanent, his eye would be returned. And do you know what the wicked brother said?"

Bud turned back to meet my gaze. I could see a smirk twisting his lips, could feel one touching mine.

"If I know him," I said, "I'll bet he told them they could keep the god-damned eye."

"He told them they could keep the god-damned eye," Bud said. "Exactly."

"And that's the story?"

"That's the story."

"I'll remember it."

Bud shrugged.

❄❄❄

Meredith and I were married — Bud came to the wedding, and seemed to enjoy watching me grind my teeth as he kissed the bride.

My kids are crazy about Bud, but I won't let them hang out with him. I had told Bud I'd remember the story he told me, and I've never forgotten it. Did he say the wicked brother had turned good? No, he said the brother's wickedness was no longer perfect. Not the same thing.

So, whenever one of our boys asks in the restaurant if he can stay over and do some fishing with Bud, I tell him no. When I do, I can count on looking up and seeing Bud grinning at me from across the room. He winks his good eye, the glass one glinting in the light, and nods.

The King of Cherokee Creek.

Note: "Blossom on the Water" was reprinted in Volume 5 (June 1, 1999) of Peridot Books online (http://peridotbooks.com). Peridot, a beautiful site of speculative fiction and informative non-fiction, changed its name and address to ALLEGORY (http://allegoryzine.com).

The Slaying of the Dragon
Jeannine Baumgartle

Ella hauled her thick black legs toward the sofa, barely lifting her feet from the floor because of the weight dragging at her hip sockets. "Like rowing a boat through mud," she mumbled, rocking a little to facilitate the momentum. Sweat stung her eyes and dampened the neckline of her old orange caftan as she focused in, headed for the splayed gold of dragon slung across the couch. Nothing mattered, not the week's worth of dirty dishes stacked on the counter behind her, or the laundry piled in the corner of the bedroom so that the door no longer opened all the way. It was her down time. —At least she'd remembered her medicine today.

Danged coffee table blocked her access (she always intended to move it) and she turned sideways, steaming and huffing, legs creased by the edge of the table as she aimed her backside for the gold haunches and collapsed heavily. Her upper torso reclined against gravity, her lower half rolling in compliance with such leverage onto the couch.

Then there was the long wait till her body adjusted to the new position, the press on the lungs lifted somewhat, and her heartbeat moved out of her ears. She lay there, one heavy arm across her pumping chest, the dragon throw beneath her all gold and red and matted into creases from years of being mashed. Her husband had mailed her the heavily embroidered piece twenty-three years ago from Indonesia, and she'd draped it proudly across the couch

. . . the dragon throw beneath her all gold and red and
matted into creases from years of being mashed.

and showed it to everybody who came. —That was before he decided to stay overseas and marry some child street-walker he'd met. The old resentment surfaced like a dark cloud. Left her there alone, with the little boy he'd never seen; her son, cheated out of a father.

She shifted her weight, struggling for something less binding to her inside arm, the one pinned against the couch, even that small exertion something to rest up from. The dragon's head was beside hers, the gold thread heavy as scales, its bared teeth and green eyes furious to get away. "Tough luck," she murmured, as much to herself as to it, and gave in to the merciful dimness of sleep.

Woke, chilled in the damp places and hot on the side up against the couch. Someone was getting into the house, the door-knob turning in place. . . .

"Mom . . . it's us . . ." (her daughter-in-law's hesitant intrusion) followed by her son's gentle prompting, "She's probably resting; it's okay — go on in."

Emma watched them enter from the hallway, the ever-so-new young couple, slender, wide-eyed, poised like deer emerging from a thicket.

"How are you, Mama?" Jordan looked at her out of his father's eyes. His wife, Signie, tugged unobtrusively at his sleeve and pointed toward the kitchen sink, so he'd know she was going to do dishes. He nodded and kissed her lightly, and returned his attentiveness to his mother.

"Good, good," Emma assured him, pulling herself to a sitting position and reaching out her arms for a hug. She patted his back, and patted a place for him to sit, not really surprised that he excused himself to throw in a load of laundry before coming back to it.

"Now Mama, what have you been up to?" he asked, leaning into the conversation as though the Ladies' Aid was something he really needed to catch up on.

They talked for a few minutes, the dishes clanking softly in the background. There was absolutely no reproach in the way they took care of her, but she felt it just the same, having her filth handled by those bright young beings with so much more in their lives that they could be doing. She had wanted to protest, but the decision was made and expedited in an instant.

Signie joined them quietly when she was finished.

"Signie has a new job," her husband bragged. "It doesn't start till after New Year's but then she'll be a junior in an accounting firm. Isn't that great?"

"It sure is," Emma bubbled for them, offering an embrace to Signie, who got up and accepted it immediately.

It gave Ella great pleasure to be family with these children, to have their love and respect. A little shiver of freedom and fear went through her. That ugly old dragon beneath her knew what Jordan's daddy was like, how he took what he wanted and left a trail of unhappiness behind him, would like to have drawn the son into the same trap, but it was too late now. Jordan was whole. He believed in life and in himself. Ella shifted her backside on the hind talons. No way all that sorrow and hardship was going to take anybody else with it. She smiled at the luxury of knowing that. Listened and watched to make sure of it.

Her son visited the restroom, and left Signie alone with her, a small figure in the over-stuffed chair. The girl listened, attentive, bright-eyed to the little tale she told of Jordan's childhood, how she'd taken him to be baptized and he'd wanted to be "good-tized" instead. Signie chuckled softly, when she got it.

"Is that true?" she asked Jordan, as he came around her chair and perched on it's upholstered arm. "That you were 'good-tized' rather than 'bad-tized?'" she clarified the joke for him.

"Oh, yes," he laughed, ducking a little at the shared glance between the two women, a little female bonding over a man's discomfort. It made Emma supremely happy and vaguely let down at the same time to realize how much had slipped by her in her own brief married life. Had her mother-in-law meant anything to her? She didn't remember.

Then it was over, they were getting up to leave.

Ella got up too, wanting to find something to send with them, apples, candy, something. Signie stared past her at the couch she'd just vacated. "You know, that's a very nice piece. . . ."

A little dismay had slipped through the cracks of her compliment.

"Would you . . . like to have this cleaned?" she offered, still eyeing the gold swirls clinging hopelessly to the back of the couch.

"I . . ." Emma couldn't think what "I" wanted to say. No dragon on the couch was beyond her imagination.

"Are you sure it can be cleaned?" Jordan offered, checking the fringed corners for a label. "Oh, yes; here it is — dry clean only. Sure. We can do that."

He bundled it into Signie's arms and they were off, waving, pulling out of the drive. Emma stared after them awhile and then pushed the door closed and went back inside.

The room looked different without its centerpiece. She'd forgotten how gentle and peaceful it was. The sofa was such a nice shade of rose; now the moss and rose floral of the chairs belonged with it. The beige rug was just a beige rug. No secrets, no past. She left it like it was a child sleeping and went about her day.

The bedroom got to be a tiresome place over the next few days. She did the laundry so she could stand to be in there, and put a doorstop in front of the door. Curtains needed washed too. Couldn't lay there only so long without seeing things.

The living room was easy to dust now. It had nothing to say.

Emma wiped the dust off the T.V., the magazine stand, the desk; watched the motes dance in the morning sun.

Her son called to find out how she was doing. "I just remembered to leave that sofa-cover off this morning," he apologized. The man said it'll be another week before he gets it back. Is that okay — I mean are you doing okay without it?"

"Doing fine," she told him, and realized it was true. More than true. It was like it was in the beginning, all her hopes and dreams intact. Busy though, lots of things to do. The house was still one step ahead of her, but she'd catch up . . . "Tell you what, honey, why don't you just keep that beast. I've got more blankets and spreads than I know what to do with."

A hesitant "Are you sure, Mama?"

"Jordan, take my word for it; I'm not missing it at all.

I'm kind of glad for the change," she told him honestly and he let it go.

It was weeks before she found time to go over to see them, what with her walking and the part time job. Dorie, next door, walked with her every day at the mall — they were up to two miles a day now — and three afternoons a week Ella worked at the children's museum. She was down to a size 18 now, and almost, on occasion, felt — alright — not winded or weary. True, there had been that dream. In the middle of the night she'd sat up in bed, the fabric dragon coming to get her, red-eyed, gold threads glinting in the dark, but the bed moved itself out the way and the fringed blanket passed on by her out into the moonlit night.

❋

Perhaps it had taken longer than it should have for her to visit the children, but she'd got here herself, without help. She looked into the little glass peephole in the door, laughed a little and pressed the bell.

Signie had excellent taste. Their apartment had all kinds of artistic stuff in it, placed just-so. The throw Emma had given them was draped across an old chest, diagonally so that the carving underneath it would show. It had no past here. It was just another nice thing.

Signie and Jordan fussed over her, exclaiming over her new hairdo — a short-short cut, sculpted around her head — and her clothes, and all she could think about all night was having fun.

The Dragon Within
Glenda Mills

The dragon within
Shields itself with heavy scales
Protected from pain
Unable — unwilling to feel
Knowing the price of vulnerability.

The dragon within
Hoards its treasures
Wealth, power, love
Relinquishes nothing
Fearing the chance of loss.

The dragon within
Sets itself high above
Sharp words from a fiery tongue
Judgement falls
Condemning its own transgressions.

The dragon within
Preying on the innocent
Those it does not know or understand
Sharp talons
Tearing merciless at the flesh.

The dragon within
Slumbers undisturbed
Safe in its power
The image of my darkness.

Buenos Noches
Marla Bilbrey

Talk about fast foods! Never in my life have I seen such a horse! Danged thing about took the food supply away. I tried telling my ignorant and apathetic best (only) friend Spark about this. He looked at me and said, "I didn't know that. Now that I do, I don't care." I have to explain something to him two-three times before he begins to understand. After I am finished, he asks, "What do you mean?" So, I'll tell you about my discovery!

It's neat how technology has advanced in the years since Man was created. In the GOOD OLD DAYS, Man came in the barest of packaging. In some ways that can be good: it is less garbage to throw away. I never had garbage duty when I was a hatchling. We now have to deal with the CUMULATIVE EFFECT OF FUNGICIDAL TREATMENT, or things that you pile up. It's a new development we must teach our children. The maidens and young are not a garbage problem.

But I digress. . .back to man. During leaner times, we had to eat the scrawny young they deliver. After cooking, the outer wrappings just burn up. One puff of breath and the ash falls off. Unfortunately, if one blasts too hard with the fire, you get New Orleans Creole cooking, or a charred crispy meal. For those that like charcoaled foods, this might not be too bad.

To illustrate the strength of the average Dragon's breath, I must tell the story of Holocaust. One day he was standing by the Man's cotton field. The pine trees were about as tall as he was, lining the Eastern border of the fields. Holocaust has an allergy problem. The pollen was heavy from his stomping through the fields. He took a deep breath, and sneezed! The air shot right through the firs, sending needles flying through the cotton fields. When the blast of snot and saliva stopped, there at the edge of the field were garments made for the Mans.

New technology has been great. Man now comes with two courses. The horse is one. Plus, the Man now comes packaged in its own foil wrapper. I really think this was an invention of my mother's. She was always onto me to exercise more. Interesting that with all her prodding, we now have FAST FOODS. Hah Mom. Cute. I've lost 500 pounds this year. Mom can be like fertilizer. Every so often she comes around and defecates on us to help us grow.

Near the mountain we have our garden. We call it a Man village. Man comes here, to scratch the ground to grow tiny rows of things to eat, yet we notice the rabbits get the vast majority of the foods. Man also scurries around, sticking small sticks into the ground to corral other small animals (I have figured out one by-product of raising cattle is calves). Durndest sight I have ever seen. It's interesting to watch them so intent on fattening themselves up on such fare as this. Some of us insist on eating Man that only eats vegetables, says it gives the meat a special flavor. Others, like me can tell no difference. Holocaust insists he can smell a Man cooking and tell if it was fed on all vegetables, meat, or both. One day, when I think of it, I will watch one particular Man that I know is a veggie eater only, cook it for Holocaust and see if he can tell. If he can, I'll swear he

was wrong . . . but that's another story.

I can pretty much tell which set of shelters harbor the most Mans. The half circular shapes with grass roofs usually hold a family of two or more. I have found two grown Mans and some of their offspring in these corrals. These are easy to get access to. Some of us like to lift the cover and then pluck them up. The disadvantages to this — they can scurry away. Face it, there are easier ways to get them, if one ain't a connoisseur of expert cooking. I prefer to give the shelter a blast, and then pick through the remains for the meat. A good washing gets rid of the grit, then one can cook more if tartar is not to one's liking. Heck, Man can be eaten raw and taste fairly good. Some Dragons say Man tastes like chicken. I think they were just down in the mouth myself.

Other Mans live in a habitat made of hard wooden planks. These are usually rectangular in shape, with many other square places sectioned off. Many of us cannot pick these up and a blast of breath can start a fire that would burn the meat way too much. The best way to get the Man out of this shelter is to have another Dragon help. One Dragon on each side of the building. At the count of three, we smash the shelter and sort through the splinters to find the meat. Pull the slivers of wood from the flesh, wash and eat.

***

Holocaust caught a Man last week. Me, Embers, Spark, Torch and Inferno were having a marshmallow roast. Embers, being afraid of fire, cowered behind the beech tree most of the night while I passed her nice toasties every so often. A gentleman goes to great lengths for his lady.

Anyway, Holocaust walks up to us, patting his belly all the while.

"I gots me a man today," he said.

"Where did you find him?" I asked.

"Oh, about over there," he said waving his arm towards the left.

"Could you see him from where you are standing now?" asked Spark.

"I could see his head," replied Holocaust.

"Where was his head?" Embers asked, jumping up and down.

"Weelll, it was right above his shoulders." said Holocaust.

"Oh, yeah? How much did he weigh?" asked Inferno.

"Guess" he said.

"Ah, about 200 pounds." I stated.

"No, guess," he said again.

Sparks hollered out "300! I say 300!"

"Nope. Guess".

By this time we all had enough of the GUESSING GAME, and frankly with no prizes being offered there was no need to continue. We all yelled, "THEN WHAT!"

"I dunno, I didn't weigh him."

❋

Ah, back to horses and FAST FOODS. A new menu item is Man On A Horse. I don't know exactly how this came to be. Mom says I am "accident prone," that I keep bumping into progress. One day, this new delicacy came into the garden. I couldn't believe my eyes! I saw a horse (which tastes better with the hair removed), and something that glinted sitting on the horse's back. In one of the thing's

"I gots me a man today," he said.

shining appendages was a long metal probe. I wasn't sure what that was for, but figured if I caught it, Mom would know. The trick was keeping them in as original shape as possible, so she could see all the packaging.

Now, comes the FAST FOOD part. Stomach rumbling, gastric juices spewing, I ran. Uphill. I swear, I have told the others that these trails need to be redone. Who ever heard of making a trail go uphill anyway? The thought "The general direction of the Alps is straight up" flashed though my mind. I crashed through a few trees. How was I to know that this THING had ears? It heard me and took off. I discovered that in places where trails do not exist, this needs to be marked. I found myself locationally challenged. It didn't matter. I might have been lost, but was still making pretty good time. Mom said I should have studied Pathology. I can only counter with the fact that I was studying those paths very intensely! BOY! Can that horse move! The silver attachment hit that horse, and the horse reared up and took off like lightening! I was not motivated by having my ideas challenged. All I knew to do was to scratch my head. Mom told me that all was not lost; I started out with nothing and had most of it left.

I went and got Inferno to come and see this marvel, cautioning him to just observe. Bad choice. He is so stubborn and tight, that when he passes gas, only dogs can hear him break wind. Guess how he got HIS name? Blasted that horse and the silver morsel before I could say no. Whatever that silver coating was, melted all over the meat. The horse was too crispy for my taste, and I think Inferno discovered that the silver stuff makes good fillings for the craters in his teeth. I considered this a waste of good food.

I invited Holocaust and Gehanna to witness another one I found. Without going into details, about the same thing happened. It was "burgicide" for sure. You know, where the meat can't take any more torture and hurls itself into the flames. Mom keeps telling me the saying is not, "Every clod has a silver lining," although, if she saw what I did, she'd understand where I got that idea.

I knew this silvery thing had something to do with Man. I could smell Man in that foil. I just didn't know how to catch this NEW Man without damaging it before we could figure out how to cook it. I finally realized that I could separate it from the horse and capture both for supper.

The problem was in "how". I asked Embers to join me in a "brain-storming-session". Very bad choice of consultants. She is afraid of fire. If you can imagine living with a Dragon that is afraid of fire, which we "fire-breathing dragons" have lots of, you'd see the problem. Also, She does not eat FAST FOODS, only turtles. It's not that she's lazy, she just likes doing research. The report she is doing now is on inertia. Mom likes her, says she isn't very smart but can lift heavy things. Embers is the only Dragon I have ever met that has pimples. She uses purple Oxydol on her eruptions. Well, I asked her to the observation meeting and she replied she couldn't, she wasn't qualified. Talk about an "Oxymoron." So, what does that make me?

I did like the advice Torch gave me.

I went to visit him after I had consulted with the others. He asked me how my Man garden was doing. I told him pretty well, considering. I have to agree with his advice, "It ain't what you know, it's what you do. It isn't what you are raising, it's all got to do with what you do with what you raise." Torch isn't very smart, according to Dragon standards. He can't figure math, or speak Man's language, but he raises excellent Mans. It's hard to argue with logic such as that.

Not being able to figure out an intelligent way to grab this Man, I decided that I'd just go for it. A Dragon's gotta do what a Dragon's gotta do, even if he has no idea of what he is doing. The game was easy to spot. The black stallion carried the silver-coated confection up the hill. I could watch their progress pretty well, the sun was out full force that day, and the creature glinted through the maples. I figured I'd just stand behind a tree and grab them as they went by.

Here they came. The Man thingy was singing some sort of ditty while the horse clomped in tune. Closer, closer, don't breathe, GRAB! That horse shot away when I lunged for it, and the Man struck me with his long silver stick. The sky was falling. . . . No. Wait. I was just tipping over backwards! I went rolling down that hillside. In retrospect, I think I'd rather climb UP the Alps than roll down them. The race was on. The dinner kept one step ahead of my rolling body as we all headed down the hillside. As I was tumbling, something caught my eye . . . and dragged it fifteen feet. I didn't feel too well being a new trail blazer that day. Trees collapsed as I made my way down. As I neared the bottom of the incline, my hunter instincts took over. Hitting a rock, I ricocheted on the meal. Caught it!

I brought Mom home all the parts; the shiny figure, horse, metal probe, and a slightly flat metal oval shaped "plate." The edges were slightly rounded up. We thought it was a bowl, but it wobbles too much to hold liquids. Mom placed it all on the cave floor, staring at it for a long time.

She tried to pick off the foil with her nails. No good. She broke her nail, ruined her manicure. She tried biting it. Said it tasted weird, and introduced a few new words to our vocabulary. Some I won't say here, but one is "metallic". Another word, "sob" if all capitalized, a period after each letter, does not mean she was crying.

Mom held up the metal probe, turning it around several times. While in thought, she picked her teeth a time or two with it. She played with the disk shape. Realization struck!

Picking up the horse, she quartered it. She took the probe and arranged the horse, vegetables, and Man (Sir Robert?????), exclaiming "SHISH-KA-BOB!" Giving a medium-rare blast she roasted the food. Sliding the pieces off she grabbed the dulled metal figure. She took her nail and found that the foil separated to reveal the meat inside. Nice red, juicy flesh. Cooked it in it's own packaging to retain the moisture for a delicacy we relished. It even came with it's own serving dish. Who could ask for more? I could. I took part of the Four Seasons: salt, pepper, mustard and vinegar. All's well that ends with a good meal.

Nede

Jeannine Baumgartle

Left this first day
in the dense forest
by my creator, I
take in the color,
find on my torso
and limbs each leafy
shade and hue, gradated
into iridescence, (caves tell
nothing of this) examine
the variegation of claw,
careful of the low
bough, the twigged nest
full of chirps.
Water in the distance.
Crawling toward it
I discover furred creatures
that burrow and climb
and hunt; winged creatures
—like me, only fragile
and short-lived.

I study them briefly,
observe the measure of
deference, the margin of
understanding each requires.
Emerge into light . . . confront
    a small human
my red eyes to his blue
        sun to sea
I love him already
        fly him
    to his people,
startled, gracious,
 urging me to stay.
    We have tea.

Sometimes Da Dragon Wins
Ginny Fleming

Krael was in a quandary. Not that I'd even laid a finger on the precocious red-haired freckled-faced palace page. Nay! I, Ben-Ally, skilled apprentice to Master Magician Seferous, was engaged in a spirited game of Demon-Tiddly-Winks with the younger lad. The beautiful courtyard of the Tyghtwhad Palace was the chosen competition field. On this lovely evening, the sun hung onto the horizon like a tenacious hyperactive Chihuahua. I love evenings like this.

The object of the habit-forming game (of which Yours Truly holds the title of Grand Champion three years running — some years running very fast!), is to flip a tiny iridescent disc into the air, using the corner of a midnight-black circlet fashioned from a gnome-fired tongue of a pissed-off gargoyle. Said multi-faceted disc spins and twirls, tumbling many times (actually 13 times — I've counted), catches the light, prisming rainbow colors over the players' intent faces, before transforming magically into a tiny demon. A tiny demon with an attitude. For some mysterious reason, the pink one with the purple polka-dots is the meanest. Why? I dasn't even make a guess. Mayhaps because he's had the misfortune to be christened: "Bruce". I've heard tell life is hard for purple polka-dotted pink demons named Bruce.

But, alas. I have strayed from the rules of the game. Let's recap. Flip pretty disc with fearsome black disc. . . . Pretty disc spins and twirls in air. . . . Changes into irate

demon. . . . Yep. That 'bout covers it. . . .Oh, yeah. I forgot to add; the micro-second the pretty circlet transforms into the tiny demon, one must invoke the name of the snarling creature, catch his eye and wink.

Hence, a typical round might go something like this: Flip the disc, sending it into the air, pretty disc undergoes instantaneous change, player notes the color and identifying character features of said nasty, swiftly calls out — "Hey, Bruce!" and winks.

Simple, you snorkel? Yeah — well. Player takes a drastic penalty if the demon's eye is not caught or if the wrong name is called out. If Player is not wary, Player risks his neck. Literally.

So, Krael and I were locked in a dead heat. It was coming down to the wire — There were only three tiddlys left. I fear the game had gone badly for my younger friend. Why, he'd already suffered the embarrassment of dry scaly skin. I'm not talking some little summer fungus here. I mean to say, five tiddlys back, Krael took a penalty on a little blue fire-breathing demon. My red-haired friend failed to notice the delicate lavender and emerald tufts peeking from the growling beastie's ears. Hence, Krael called out: "Hey! Bolong-Dramling-TuTu!!" When this particular dyspeptic demon's moniker was "Leroy".

Krael spent two penalty rounds resembling a pale used-up version of Yurazz, King Radnoor's new son-in-law. Mere months before, Krael and I saw need to rescue the shape-changing dragon from the King's beautiful daughter, Princess Jasmine. To show his gratitude, the man/dragon with the brilliant criminal mind up and married the royal nymph — ahem — Princess with the healthy appetite.

"Your move," Krael growled, brimstone scented smoke tendriling from his nostrils, "Make it quick. I want to finish this game."

"Krael — Tsk-Tsk," I tsked, "Why, the game is in the playing. It matters not whether one wins or loses, only if one escapes with one's life."

"Easy for you to say," he grumbled scalishly, "You're winning. I don't see you sitting there with donkey ears, looking like an ass, or sprouting two heads like some big . . . big . . . big two-headed thingy."

I could see the stress of the game was telling on my little friend. "There, there," I said, not able to think of other soothing words, "There, there. Calm down, don't let it get to you — it's only a game!"

I made my move and flipped my tiddly. It twirled and spun, revolving the magical number of revolutions, suddenly changed into a little puke-orange nasty, and I made the call: "Hey-Hey, Phaula!" I chortled, as the tiny monster glared

my way. I flashed a winning wink and the disgruntled creature vanished from sight. So far, so good.

"Your move, Krael."

"Grrrrr," he growled. Krael's scales had by now faded until he no longer resembled a small, scaly, red-haired behemoth. Now, it seemed, he merely suffered the heartbreak of psoriasis.

"Your move, Krael." The page flipped his disc. A bright yellow nasty popped up. He had a big red nose and flaming red hair (I mean to say his hair was actually on fire!), and Krael called out: "Hey, Ronald!" He was finally getting the hang of it! — was my first thought. Drat the Demon; of all the dumb luck!! — was my next thought as disaster raised its hoary head.

Catching the demon's uncharacteristically cheerful eye, Krael made to wink and was suddenly seized by a violent and quite painful-looking eye spasm. Mayhaps a speck of dust flew into his eye — I dasn't make a wager. No matter the reason, he shut both eyes tight.

Knowing, by missing the wink, he'd suffer a penalty, the young page kept his eyes closed. "Ben-Ally?" his voice quivered, "Tell me what happened. Am I green and scaly again? Do I have antennae?"

"No. . . You have flaming red hair."

"Ben-Ally — this is not the time to jest!" Krael snapped, "Please don't be a master of the obvious!"

"No," I gently touched my friend's arm in comfort, "I mean you have flaming red hair . . . and a big round red nose . . . and a neck-to-ankle yellow suit . . . and huge red shoes . . . an—"

"Alright-Alright!" Krael grumbled, "I get the picture,"

his hair snapped, crackled and popped as the red-hot tongues licked the air, "By Gaytor, I believe I hate this game. Please slap me soundly if I ever play again. Really I think. . . ."

"Hush!"

"No, really. I—"

"Hush!" I plastered my hand across Krael's red-greasepainted lips, "I mean — listen! Do you hear that?" We must have been a sight, huddled over the game board, my hand holding in Krael's words, our ears craned for the slightest sound.

Suddenly, Krael grabbed my hand, ripped it away from his mouth, and took a deep dragging breath, "Gaytor's Euthanasia! This big red nose isn't meant for taking in air! Are you trying to kill me?!?"

A figure slunk out of the surrounding bushes, and Yurazz, in his man-form, slid up to the courtyard table, looking over his shoulder, checking to make sure he'd not been followed. "Trying to kill Krael again, I see," the mighty man/dragon rumbled, "Really, Ben-Ally — when will you ever learn? Might does not necessarily make right. That is, unless one is a dragon."

"Taking the air, Yurazz?" I growled in greeting.

"Have an vital errand to run," the blond dandy replied.

Krael's ears perked up (in his present condition, this made him appear even more clownish), "What? Is King Radnoor sending you on a righteous mission? Are you off to battle for Kingdom and King? Making a run for illegal Gnome Brew?"

"Nothing so noble," Yurazz smoldered, "Gotta get me some Grimlich."

"Grimlich?" I pondered, my faced screwed-up in deep

thought.

"Don't do that, please," the foppish blond gaggingly admonished me, "That's a face that would scare the scales right off a manly dragon. . . . Yes; indeed. I must travel to the ends of the Earth to fetch Grimlich."

"Is it a powerful ingredient needed for one of Master Seferous' magical spells?" I pondered again, careful not to ponder too deeply. Concern for Yurazz's well-being, you understand.

"No."

Krael wondered aloud, as his head extinguished itself (the penalty was running its course), "Is it a priceless golden treasure?"

"No no no. . . ."

"Is it—" I began.

"Okay, okay," Yurazz interrupted me, "You guys oughta work for the HEX-Files. You two could badger the gold fillings out of a closed-mouth gargoyle. So I'll tell ya. Grimlich is a plant."

"A plant?" I screwed-up my face again.

"Gaytor's Heartattack!" Yurazz squealed, "Let me finish! You've heard, no doubt, that Princess Jasmine is Sitting-the-Egg."

"Sitting-the-Egg?" I scratched my head. Frankly, he was losing me.

Yurazz wiped beads of sweat from his foppish brow, "Pray, allow me to spit this out quickly, before you do any more pondering. Me thinks my heart, my achy-breaky heart, just can't take any more frights. Princess Jasmine and I are to be blessed with an heir. Soon we shall hear the flapping of tiny wings. The egg shall crack and we will be the proud parents of a baby dragon . . . or dragonette."

"Dragonette?" I couldn't stop myself. Really, I thought dragonette was something one splashed on salad.

Yurazz hissed though clenched teeth, "Yes, dragonette. Princess Jasmine grows weary Sitting-the-Egg. Naturally, she has cravings. She's told me she'd kill for some Grimlich," the blond man/dragon with the Prince Valiant haircut looked up at the storm clouds gathering around the Princess' turret window and sighed, "And I truly do believe she would. So, I'm bound for Eyedaho, and Grimlich is my mission. Are you with me, lads?"

"Really?!?" Krael crowed, "You'd let us go with you?"

"Really?!?" I choked back my fear, "You'd force us to go with you?"

"Surely," the mighty man/dragon smiled. He stood back from us a safe distance and spread his silk and lace covered arms, flapping them in the breeze as he sang: "I gotta be me! I gotta be me!!" In moments, a glorious dragon stood before us with iridescent scales and multi-faceted eyes swirling rainbow prisms of color.

"Mount up." he ordered.

"Weeeee!" crowed Krael, climbing onto the mighty dragon's back.

"Oh, my mother," I wailed, "I'm going to burn!!" Reluctantly, I took my place behind the excited red-haired page.

※

The flight into Eyedaho was uneventful as such terrifying journeys go. Quite enjoyable, actually, if one enjoys being flung though the air on the back of a humongous mean-spirited dragon, flying at the speed of sound. At least, faster than the speed of my heart-rending screams of: "Oh, Gaytor!! We're gonna crash! Jeez, Oh Gaytor! What was THAT?!? Wind shear?!? Oh, Merciful Gaytor!!"

Grumbling about barbecued apprentice legs, Yurazz waited until we disembarked before stalking off to the side, where he again flapped his wings and sang: "Mucho-macho-man, I've got to be a macho-man." Soonly, the fancy-dressed blond dandy stood before us once more.

"Ready to fetch the Grimlich?" he asked, pointing to a tall tower with just one window in the top-most apartment. As one, Krael and I nodded our heads. Krael was up for the game, I just wanted this night to end. Yurazz strutted up to the base of the tower like a man on a mission (which he was), and yelled up at the apartment in the clouds: "Rapunzel, Rapunzel! Let down your hair!"

"Oky-Doky!" came a sweet, but dim, voice. And a tiny white bunny rabbit came sailing out the window. I caught the little fluffy, and gently placed it on the ground while Yurazz pinched the tiny part of his nose between his closed eyes.

"No. . . ." he called up at the tower in a purposely calm voice, "No — I believe you misunderstood me. In fact, what we have here is a failure to communicate. When I said: Rapunzel, Rapunzel let down your hair, mayhaps I should have been more specific. Let's try it again, shall we? Okay. Rapunzel, Rapunzel let down your GOLDEN hair, that I may climb your golden stair."

"Oh — Riiiight!" said the sweet voice sweetly, "The golden stair — Riiiight! Sometimes I get the two confused.

Just give me a sec." True to her word, in seconds, mounds and plaits of golden hair tumbled out the tower window, cascading to the ground at our feet.

"Lads, you first," Yurazz gestured at the beautifully well-groomed hair trailing down the tower like a Lorial-Ladder. Frankly, I was surprised they'd not thought of wooden ladders in Eyedaho, but I shrugged my shoulders and murmured to myself: "What the hay, I'm worth it." And I climbed the freshly-washed and delightfully fragrant coiffure.

Being swift of foot and strong of arm, the three of us mighty warriors reached the top of the towering tower in record time (though to be truthful nobody thought to time us), and we climbed inside the penthouse apartment and stood before a vision.

And what a vision she was! Why, I believe she might have even been naked, though, I really couldn't be sure. You see, Rapunzel was covered head to toe in plaits and curls of her tumbling golden hair. Only her beautiful face was visible, peeking out through a glorious frame of herbal-conditioned gold. I dast say she was in no need of Row-Ghain.

"Welcome to Eyedaho," Rapunzel beamed, spitting a stray clump of golden hair from her mouth, "Make yourself at home, and—"

"Zelly?!?" came a screeching voice from the corner (Wait a moment, we're in a round tower room... Where did they find a corner?) bedroom, "Zelly? Who's out there with you?"

"Visitors, Ma," Rapunzel called sweetly to her mother.

"How many times have I told you," an old green-skinned woman staggered out of the bedroom scratching her rump

and adjusting a pointy black cap on her head, "Visitors wait at the bottom of the tower. Speak to them through the door."

"We don't have a door, Ma," Rapunzel gently reminded her obviously senile mother, "and that first step sure is a doozy."

The old wart-nosed woman looked at Yurazz and harrumphed, "Harrumph, what do you want, Pretty-Boy? Come to steal Babayaga's lovely daughter away?"

"Noooooooo!" Yurazz backed frantically against the wall, his well-manicured hands held piteously out before him, "Believe me, not that! I've traveled from far and wide for one thing and one thing only. Grimlich. I'll not leave until I hold a goodly supply in my hands."

"Ahh, well. . . ." the old hag snorted (I lost my desire for a late-night snack), "I better fix up the guest room, then. You'll be here a long time. The only Grimlich left is in that pot there, in the corner."

Really, I wondered, taking care not to screw-up my face, where were they getting these corners?

"Name your price." said Yurazz, eyeing the old witch with a bargainor's eye.

"Not for sale." snarled the green-skinned Babayaga, returning Yurazz's glare.

"Flip you for it." the mighty man/dragon offered.

"Demon-Tiddly-Winks?" the old crone crowed, "I love a good game of Demon-Tiddly-Winks! Why, I just happen to have my board set up over here in the corner."

Really, where. . . . Oh, never mind.

✳✳✳

The game got off to a bad start. For Yurazz. Babayaga

was a pro. That is to say, she could have given me a run for Grand Champion of Tyghtwhad DT-Winks Semi-Annual Competition. Good thing she lived outside the eligibility limits. By the fourth round (they were playing a quick round of five), Yurazz had momentarily been a pus-oozing gargoyle, a buck-toothed giant rat, a bulbous fat yellow slug, and now he sat before us as a tall, orange-haired dark-skinned man dressed in a brightly colored shorts set complete with a massive pair of High-Tops, and a pink feather-boa draped around his shoulders. He bounced an over-sized brown ball in one hand, while wiping a thin rivulet of drool from his lip. Dribbling, I pondered. . . . Bizarre was not the word!

"Your move, Bitch! I mean . . . Witch!" he snapped, batting his fuchsia-painted eye-lids.

Babayaga laughed the laugh of the over-confident. "No Grimlich for you, Pretty-Boy!" she crowed, flipping the last disc. It spun and twirled and a tiny geeky bespectacled green, silver, and gold demon, who apparently thought he owned the world or at least held a controlling interest in it, appeared. "Hey, Bhill-Ghates!!" she cried, and my heart sank. Surely, the old green-skinned hag had won the game. And now, I would be forced to watch a mighty dragon cry.

"Think fast, Sister!" Yurazz laughed, wrapping the pink fluffy feather-boa around the startled old witch's head. Naturally, Babayaga missed the wink. Micro-seconds later, she sat before us wearing a donkey's head, complete with brown fur and the tell-tale long ears.

Newly swift of foot, she brayed like a donkey and ran to the window. Babayaga frantically yanked and twisted a long stick hanging along-side the curtains, "Open-Close-Open-Close-Open-Close — Oh, why; Oh, why won't these windows take my commands? Re-Boot — Re-Boot — Re-Boot!!!" I looked to her shoes, and shook my head confused as was my wont. I mean, I thought the purple mukluks gracing her number nines were more than adequate.

"Make haste, lads!" Yurazz cried, grabbing the Grimlich and pushing us to the hairy ladder, "We must fly! Fly like the wind! See ya, Zelly! You're a good kid! Stay away from the Winks — it's a nasty habit!" With these sage words, Yurazz pushed us out the window. Oh, Gaytor — Save us!!

※

Back at the Tyghtwhad Palace (yes, I'm as surprised as anyone we made it back safely), Yurazz hurried the prized Grimlich to the egg-sitting Princess and the storm clouds left the skies. Krael yawned and announced he was turning in for the night. I looked up at the glorious night sky, marveling at the stars twinkling overhead.

"One more game before bed?" I smiled my most winning smile.

"Slap me," Krael moaned, "Just slap me now. . . ."

Six Lies of the Dragon
Marla Bilbrey

Come here. Hold me. Now baby, I see your pain.
It's a controlling force in me, it's the dragon.
He gets mad, he rises up, out comes the fire.
I am lost in myself, controlled by the rage.
I need you now. Can't you see I need your love?
Please, don't go. Darling, this evil we will conquer.

I can't do this alone. The two of us can conquer
all the feelings of sorrow, the hurts, the pain.
I know I hurt you, yet I can't do without your love.
It's not me baby, I promise. It's the dragon.
Help me stop this inferno, the charring rage.
It consumes my every thought, a roaring fire.

See the fiery streaks? I'm enveloped in the fire.
Your love is the water, the power that will conquer.
The forceful passion that quenches that damn rage.
Oh, how I love you baby, and hate to see your pain.
Be my Knight, my damsel, slay the ugly dragon.
I know you can. We are one. I can see your love.

It soothes me. It fills me. Baby share your love.
Come, let us change the hate to a passionate fire.
Give us another chance, please to dispose of the dragon.
I'll be gentle with you. With love, we will conquer.
I'll caress you, not hit you, forever ending the pain.
We'll be happy, a once upon a time story, free of rage.

I'm afraid you'll leave, start your own rage.
I'm good for you baby, you need my love.
If you leave me, it will cause more pain
Better to stay, and quench the evil fire.
Please, don't go. Stay, don't divide, CONQUER!
Slay it! Defeat it! It's also your dragon.

Honey, I can see it. It's you, you are also the dragon.
You feel suppressed, let it out. But, not in a rage.
Use it to show me how a hero can fight, conquer.
Do it! Now! Kill it! Use your sword of love.
STAY! Shut the door. Your eyes have that fire.
This hurts, I need you. Please don't cause me pain!

(Ha! Baby! You conquer? I defeated your love.
You slew the dragon? You'll again see his rage.
I still have that fire, I'll still cause you pain).

Slaying Summer's Dragon
Dirk D. Griffin

David Scharre bounded over the small white fence and threw the full force of his eleven-year-old frame into the larger, older boy. The older boy tilted backwards, suddenly off balance, but managed to twist himself as he fell: the two forms spun round, giving advantage to Morton McNabb, the larger combatant. David flushed with renewed anger at the endangering reversal and struggled against the falling weight of McNabb's muscular body now slamming him into the lawn. The rowdy crowd around the altercation cheered at the explosion of violence. McNabb's mob, an odd collection of lower class troublemakers, shouted obscenities at David and frothed with enthusiasm for their chosen hero, McNabb.

"Punch his damn lights out!" yelled one.

"Kick 'm inna balls!" cried another.

These sounds along with others blended into a hum of white noise as David, under the weight of McNabb, felt his breath completely escape his body. Darkness inched its way around the edges of his vision and the red hair and freckles of McNabb's primitive features faded to brown.

Mitchell Bryant, formerly the object of McNabb's derision, discovered himself pushed from the fight as other children encircled and concentrated on the unevenly matched pair struggling in the grassy play area. Confused at his rapid change in fortune, Mitchell stood awestruck at the turbulent scene before him. Then, like someone waking from a deep sleep, he grasped the seriousness of the situation: McNabb could kill David as easily as other kids kill flies. Once this idea arose in Mitchell's consciousness, he turned toward the school building and moved his crippled form as quickly as he could toward the door and the teacher he hoped was just beyond.

He hadn't always been disabled. He used to be a "normal" kid — until two years earlier. That was when it happened. Mitchell's mother was returning home with him and a week's worth of groceries on a cold and icy January evening. While maneuvering the car down a troublesome, slick hill, she lost control and crashed into a small brick wall. Luckily, they only experienced bumps and bruises — however, being a frightened eight-year-old, Mitchell scrambled to get out of the car. His mother tried to stop him, but her reactions had been slowed by the crash. He jumped from the car, slipped on the ice and disappeared beneath the auto. Frantically, she opened her door. The new movement forced the car to slip further down the hill; as she listened in horror, Mitchell screamed his pain. The car slid down, crushing his knee, and demolished most of his right shin. Reconstruction and therapy allowed Mitchell to return to public school, but the brace, the horrible brace, was a constant reminder to everyone that he was now, somehow, different. That was all in the past for Mitchell as he clomped his way across the concrete recreation area.

In the war zone, David regained his breath, but only after taking two good fists across his left cheek. Pinned beneath McNabb, his injured cheek already swollen and burning red with pain and anger, David wildly reached out for something, anything to stave off the beating. Anything came in the form of a fallen branch which David shattered against McNabb's head. The surprise and pain of the moment forced McNabb to cease his assault. David took advantage of the break by pulling his limber form out from under his bulkier opponent. Once up, however, he discovered they were now surrounded by the other children who, like a Roman crowd thirsting for blood, were chanting, cheering, and barring all means of escape. One of McNabb's cronies pushed David from behind and sent him tumbling over the still groggy McNabb. Both boys collapsed into a pile, spent by the brief yet vicious outburst of violence. David rolled with the fall and rose rapidly to his feet while McNabb rolled feebly on the ground clutching his head. The boys who were helping him taunt Mitchell moved forward toward their fallen gladiator. Delbert, a short stocky boy with black, unkempt hair, and reddish skin was the first to notice:

"Oh, man!" he exclaimed, "you done got your head busted, McNabb!"

McNabb only managed a weak groan as the other children fell back, seeing the blood mixed in with Morton McNabb's reddish, long mane. Almost as one, the children gasped in fear and wonder at the bloodied bully.

Morton McNabb engendered no love among those who had the misfortune to serve time at Meinert Elementary School with him and his gang of bullies. The sight of him bloodied and beaten was almost pathetic; it was frightening in its own way. As he slowly regained himself, he rose to his full stature, nearly a foot taller than David. McNabb was nearly fourteen years old but, due to poor academic performance, was only in sixth grade. Once back on his feet, McNabb grabbed David. David struggled, but McNabb rammed his knee into David's stomach. He fell into a lump at McNabb's feet. David lay in helpless pain. McNabb kicked him with the steel-toed work boots he always wore and spat out, "You just wait Scharre, I'm gonna kill you for this."

Blood was still running down McNabb's face, framing his eyes and starting to dry in the warm late May sun. This along with his unruly and matted hair, gave him the look of a terrible mythic monster. Most all the children felt themselves take an involuntary and cautious step backwards. He turned to Delbert, his man at guard, and growled, "Let's get the hell out of here."

With that, the gang of five moved away through the rapidly parting crowd. The departure left the other children standing silent and calm, like the stillness following a tornado. David slowly sat up, pain coursing through his body. He began to assess his damage: two buttons gone, one from his shirt cuff, shirt collar ripped "—When did that happen?" He couldn't remember anything specific about the fight, just an intense fear, an intense need for survival.

Moments after the gang of bullies disappeared down the street, Mitchell returned with Mrs. Sandberg, a teacher late in her career, and veteran of many such pre-adolescent clashes.

"What happened?" she asked.

"What happened!?" The children exchanged looks with each other. "What happened?!" The words hung in the air, echoing without answer. No one could piece it together. It seemed to make no sense at all.

Finally David spoke up, "Morton and the guys were picking on Mitchell, pushing him, calling him names —

everybody was just standing around staring like . . . I don't know like they just couldn't see it happening."

Mrs. Sandberg looked down at David, his dark features attractive, but bruised, one eye swelling, a lip following suit. "And you decided," she said dispassionately, "to take matters into your own hands?"

"Well . . . yes, ma'am." David paused in thought; he looked at his feet then back up to the slightly heavy teacher. "It just didn't seem like there was time to get anyone — another minute and they woulda been all over him."

"I see," she said. "Come with me and we'll see if the school nurse is still available." With that pronouncement, she led David back into the building — the other children staring in disbelief and silence. One of them finally said, "What a heck of a way to start the summer."

These words broke the pall that had hung over them and they began to disperse into their smaller, familiar cliques. Mitchell returned to the school building with David and Mrs. Sandberg. A silent procession marking the close of another year of school.

A short time later, the two boys sat like mismatched bookends on the wooden bench outside of Principal Beryl's office. Mitchell, at his end, stared at the black and white pattern that covered the floor. His body slumped forward and down to better examine the flow of black diamonds versus the flow of white diamonds. He was trying very hard not to think of the recent events that placed him here. David, at his side, sat with his head back, eyes closed, and one hand holding an ice bag on the more bruised side of his face. His concentration wasn't on the dotted ceiling tiles or why he was here. He was trying hard not to feel the pain burning his cheek.

From within Beryl's office, the boys could faintly hear the discussion between Mrs. Sandberg and the Principal.

"They're both good boys, Jim, I really don't think that they should be blamed in this."

"Just the same," said Beryl, "We can't condone fighting as a solution to problems."

"So that's it. You're going to punish the victims and leave the attacker alone?" Ann Sandberg looked down at the seated principal. He took a breath and removed his glasses, revealing a kind of weariness. He was looking forward to summer and a respite from situations like this.

"No," he said, "I can't punish them for standing up for themselves and McNabb is free for the summer. I think I would like to talk to the boys though, give them some perspective on this."

"What about the McNabb boy? Isn't there something we can do? He's been a terror all year long."

"I'm at a loss. I've suspended him three times this year. I've spoken with his parents numerous times. Frankly, I think his home life may be contributing to the problem, but once they're off school grounds, we have no authority over them. If his parents won't cooperate, then he'll always be a problem." Beryl paused a moment reflecting on the situation and taking in the general concern that Mrs. Sandberg had for it. "If it will make you feel better, I can send another letter to Morton's parents."

"Yes, it would," she responded quickly. "I don't think it will help, but it would make me feel better."

"Well, I guess you can send them in, I'll take care of the rest of it if you want to go on home."

"Thanks, Jim, you won't regret it. I'll send them right in." She turned to go and then turned back. "Oh, by the way, have a good summer."

"I intend to do just that, Ann. Thanks." As she left, he straightened his tie and put on his best stern principal face.

Quietly and cautiously, the door opened. David entered first, an ice bag still held to his face, with Mitchell trudging slowly behind. Beryl rose to the full height of his Lincolnesque form, cleared his throat, and spoke:

"Come in," he began in a firm deep voice. "Close the door and have a seat." David closed the door and both boys sat in the two large, dark, wooden chairs that stood before the principal's desk.

"I understand that you've been fighting," he said, looking back and forth between the two boys.

"Actually," Mitchell interrupted, "I was just getting beat up, sir. David's the only one who really got to fight."

"Great going Mitchell," whispered a slightly irritated David.

Beryl suppressed a smile and commented, "Oh, I see." He turned to fully face both boys now. "How long has Morton been beating you up Mitchell?"

Mitchell gave the question serious thought before speaking: "Well, I guess I'd say he's been doing it ever since I got here, sir."

"You mean to tell me that ever since you arrived in January, this has been going on?"

"W-w-well, yes, sir . . . as best I can figure."

"Why in heaven's name haven't you said anything to anybody about this?"

Mitchell sat silent, his answer stuck in his throat. Jim

Beryl could see the ghost of fear or confusion in the boy's eye; he walked around his desk and kneeled beside him. "Mitchell, it's okay, I'm here to help you," he said gently.

David spoke up, "He didn't want any trouble, sir."

Beryl looked across to Mitchell's black and blue protector. "Didn't want trouble?" he said, trying to understand. "What do you call being assaulted on a regular basis?"

"You don't understand . . . ." David explained.

"A guy can't rat on another guy." Mitchell practically shouted.

Stunned by the sudden outburst, both David and Beryl looked at Mitchell who was almost in tears. "A guy can't rat on another guy," he repeated through his tears, "even if the other guy's just some old dragon!" David moved over toward Mitchell and instinctively put a hand on his shoulder. He had watched McNabb's systematic abuse of Mitchell over the six weeks he had been at the school. Watched Mitchell surrender money, sandwiches, baseball cards, even a yo-yo to McNabb and his band of crooks. Today was just the last one he could watch without doing something.

"Now, Mitchell," said Beryl, "Morton's just another boy, he's no dragon."

"Yes he is!" insisted Mitchell. "He comes in and picks on people smaller than him, and takes all their stuff and keeps it for himself — he's a big red dragon."

Beryl reached for some facial tissues on his desk and handed it to Mitchell. "Now son, there's no reason to be so upset by it all. I tell you what I'm going to do."

"What?" said Mitchell between abating sobs.

"I'm going to take you both home myself — and maybe we can get some ice cream on the way." For all his posturing, Jim Beryl was as soft as they came. "I'll take them home, speak to the parents about it and let them know I intend to contact the McNabbs," he thought.

"Wow!" exclaimed David, "Ow!" his outburst renewing the pain in his jaw.

"Don't think of this as a reward for fighting, think of it as an incentive to look for better solutions next time," said Beryl.

After a phone call to the parents to explain the situation they were off. Three chocolate sodas and a short ride later, the trio found itself at the Bryant home. Principal Beryl spoke with Mrs. Bryant in the house, leaving David and Mitchell alone to amuse themselves in the back yard.

Exploring the swings on the yard set, Mitchell spoke up for the first time: "I want to thank you for what you did," he said earnestly. David shrugged as if to say "no big deal," but Mitchell couldn't leave it at that. "No, really, I mean thank you, you didn't have to do anything about it, but you did."

"I should've done something sooner. It's not right he should do that to anybody, especially you."

"I guess," said Mitchell. "I'm just no good at fighting. Leastways, not like you."

"Me? Good at fighting?" asked a surprised David. Mitchell bobbed his head up and down. "Well . . . I guess I do okay. You know this is my fifth school in two years. We keep moving," he explained. "I've had to do a lot of fighting 'cause they always want to ride the new kid. I didn't have that problem when I came here, though — they were always picking on you."

"Boy, were they ever," said Mitchell, and both boys shared a brief laugh.

After a moment David confessed, "I guess I didn't do anything before because I was glad they weren't messing with me. It felt good to come to a school and not have to fight."

Mitchell considered these words for a moment and then slapped David on the back. "Don't let it bother you," he said, "he's just an old Smaugified dragon anyway."

David looked directly into Mitchell's eyes. "You've said that before, 'he's a dragon' — what does that mean?"

"It's all in the book," explained Mitchell.

"Book?"

"Yeah, The Hobbit, you've read that, haven't you?"

"No, I haven't. I'm, uh, not much of a reader."

"Oh, man, I can't believe this." Mitchell stood up and hobbled to a medium sized tent in one corner of his back yard. "He hasn't read it, I can't believe it," he was mumbling to himself, "just the greatest book ever written and he hasn't read it!"

David followed, but not too close, unsure what to make of Mitchell's strange behavior. Mitchell disappeared into the tent and it came alive with activity. There was banging and the sides of the tent bulged with occasional movement all the while Mitchell continued mumbling to himself. Suddenly, with a shout of "Got It!" the movement ceased, and Mitchell emerged from the tent. He presented a small faded paperback book, dog-eared and worn from overuse. "This is it!" he gleamed. "My dad read it to me first, but I've read it a few times myself since then."

"What's so great about it?"

"What's so great about it!?"

"Yeah, why is it the GREATEST book in the world and why does it make McNabb a dragon?"

"Okay, it's about this wizard that gets a hobbit—"

"Hobbit, what's that?"

Rapidly, Mitchell provided his answer, "They're some of the smallest people in the world and they kinda live underground. Anyway, he takes him on a quest to help the King of the Dwarves get back his kingdom and all his treasure. Only, when they get there, the dwarves won't help and the hobbit, his name's Bilbo, has to go get it all back."

David was dizzy from the explanation. "So?"

"Sooo he does it. He kills the dragon and saves everybody."

"Oh," said David, "and so all we need to keep McNabb from picking on us is one of the hobbits, right?"

"Don't be silly, hobbits aren't real. It's just because Smaug is a great, red, bullying, stinker that's why I started thinking of McNabb as a dragon."

"Okay, now I get it," said David. "I guess it does sound pretty cool at that. You think if I come over sometime we could look at that book?"

"Hey, you don't have to come over, you can borrow it."

David looked uneasy. "I can't."

"What do you mean you can't — here I'm loaning it to you."

"Now you don't understand," countered David.

"Huh?"

"I'm not much of a reader 'cause I can't read much."

"Oh . . . you mean . . ."

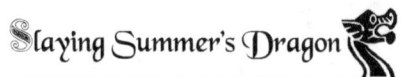
"Yeah, I mean."

Mitchell paused a moment. "Well, hey, I'll make a deal with you."

"What?"

"If you come over and teach me how to fight, I'll help you read this book."

"Really?" said David.

"Hey, really, you think I like being pushed around all the time?"

"Well . . . no. Okay, I'll ask my Mom when I get home today."

At that moment, Mrs. Bryant and Principal Beryl appeared at the back door.

Mrs. Bryant called out, "David, it's time to go now."

"Okay," answered David and he started to go. "Wait!" he exclaimed and turned to Mitchell. "How'm I going to tell you if it's okay?"

"Here, take the book — it's got my phone number in it."

David snatched the book and headed for the house, turning only briefly to wave at his new friend.

✳✳✳

The deal couldn't have gone better for both boys. The first weeks of summer were full of the exhilaration that comes when youth experiences freedom. The mothers were both glad to have the boys spend time with one another and the boys, though seemingly unmatched, clicked well together. David, who was not given to academics, found himself introduced to it in a new way through Mitchell's enthusiasm. David, on the other hand, refused to let Mitchell use his brace as an excuse not to have fun physically. Not only did they work on reading, but also baseball, bug and rock collecting, basketball, and chess.

Every couple of days, David rode the two of them over to the park on his bike. Once there, they looked for rocks and bugs for their collections. It was on one such trip, at the end of the first month of summer vacation that McNabb re-entered their lives.

Their favorite spot for searching was a hill that fell down into a creek. It was only about twenty-five feet long and the angle wasn't too steep, fifty-five or sixty degrees. With David's help Mitchell became proficient at searching the lower areas, while David played the daredevil searching the upper reaches. That particular afternoon David climbed nearly to the top, while Mitchell remained at the bottom looking for bugs around the creek. The creek wasn't formidable by any means, only seven or eight feet across and no more than a foot deep at its lowest point. The water flowed smoothly and evenly, swirling around a few larger rocks and some fallen tree limbs. David was concentrating on digging out a large stone containing a fossil impression when he heard a sound. It sounded like metal being dragged around roughly. He looked down and could see Mitchell wading in the stream near a fallen limb about ten yards further down. He looked back from the direction he came and there was the source of his sound. McNabb and some of his cronies were dragging, not carrying, dragging David's bicycle toward the creek. Without thinking, he was scaling down the rocky hillside toward the scene.

"Hey, Sharre!" McNabb yelled up. "This is just for starters!" That was the cue: three of McNabb's toughs heaved the bike into the air sending it splashing into the deepest part of the water. They all were laughing as David increased his pace down the hillside. After David reached the halfway point, McNabb gave a sign to the others and they exited laughing. McNabb turned and shouted back at David, "You're next. You remember that. You're next!" By the time David reached the base of the hill they were too far away to follow. He fished his Huffy Special out of the water and inspected it for damage. A couple of spokes were bent, but nothing that couldn't be fixed.

David walked the bike down to where he last saw Mitchell: "It's all clear, Mitchell, you can come out now," David said with slight irritation. Mitchell presently appeared, from behind a nearby tree, looking somewhat dejected.

"You know Mitchell, if we don't stand up to him, he's just going to keep this up."

"Yeah, I know."

"Well, I guess you know that means hiding behind trees isn't standing up to him, then, right?"

"Yeah, it's just I don't feel ready to stand up to him. Can't you show me some more about fighting?"

"Mitchell, I've told you everything I know except one thing."

"What's that?" Mitchell brightened.

"If all else fails, get something big and hit 'em with it."

Mitchell looked puzzled, then said, "Big. Like what?"

"Like a stick, a rock, anything that can help."

"Well, I guess so," said Mitchell.

"Don't guess so, know so."

"Okay, I'll do it." he said with more conviction.

"Great!" said David, feeling like he'd accomplished something. "I guess we should go and look at what we've got — and maybe straighten the spokes out on my bike." Gathering their booty, they climbed aboard the bike and returned home. David was slightly distracted during the trip, concentrating on McNabb's having taken the time to hunt him down. "That can't be a good thing," he thought. "Especially since I've never seen him outside of school."

Concern followed him through cataloging rocks and bugs, home, and dinner. The comfort of home couldn't make up for the violation he felt at being sought out by McNabb. He tried to relax by reading, which the more he did, the less of a chore it seemed to be, but finally decided on sleep.

Sleep itself proved no respite and was invaded by reality and unreality. David dreamed that he was in the park collecting rocks with Mitchell when McNabb showed up. McNabb's gang attacked. Mitchell and David beat them off — with large sticks. McNabb flared with anger at the defeat. He yelled curses at the boys. With each curse, he changed little by little into a great red dragon. The dragon swept Mitchell aside with his tail. When David looked back at his stick, it had become a sword. He rushed forward to the dragon, and was swallowed whole by it. His last memory upon waking was the feeling of falling eternally into a pit of fire. He eventually returned to an uneasy sleep and the remainder of the night was unrestful.

At breakfast he had little appetite as he pondered the situation. "Maybe he'll get bored with it and forget the whole thing. Right," he thought to himself, "and Mom and Dad are going to forget my history grade too — I'm still doing chores for that one and it's been over a month." A few bites of his eggs, a few drinks of milk later, he was still stuck on what to do: "Maybe Dad will get transferred again, real soon." That prospect brightened him for all of thirty seconds — he couldn't believe he was happy at the thought of moving again — until he realized that would only make things worse for Mitchell. He finished breakfast, said his goodbyes, and headed for Mitchell's hoping that two heads would be better than one.

His arrival at Mitchell's did nothing to cheer him. During the night, someone had shredded the backyard tent with a knife and strewn Mitchell's possessions all over the yard and down the street. Mitchell's mother was distraught and Mitchell himself was involved in gathering and accounting for all the missing items. David started helping with the reclamation process.

"McNabb, right?" he asked in between Lincoln Logs.

"What do you think?" Mitchell shot back angrily.

"I've been thinking about this a lot and . . ." he paused, looking for the right words.

"Yeah, me too," Mitchell interjected into the silence.

"Well, what do you think?" asked David warily.

"I was hoping you had an idea," was the flat reply.

"I don't much like my idea."

"Which is what?"

"Well . . . ."

"Come on, spit it out!" Mitchell demanded.

"Okay, I think we should slay the dragon."

"What?"

"I think we should—"

"I heard what you said!"

"Then why—"

"We can't kill him, are you crazy?"

"Well, I think he's going to kill us."

"I don't think so — maybe we'd wish we were dead, but he wouldn't kill us." They continued gathering the books, pencils, pads, action figures and other items in silence, weighing their options. In between trips to the back porch and down the street Mitchell had an inspiration. "I know!" he shouted. "I-know-I-know-I-know!" He began jumping up and down in an awkward motion.

"Well, tell me!" pleaded David.

"What gives a dragon his power?" A smile of absolute victory shone through the question.

"His power?" David thought for a moment. "Gee, I always thought it was because he could beat everyone up."

"Exactly," said Mitchell. "And why can he do that?" David stared blankly at him. Finally, in exasperation, Mitchell told him: "Because everyone fears him."

"So he can beat people up because they're afraid of him?"

"Well, sort of. Yes, he's bigger and stronger than everyone, but part of that is everyone thinks he's unbeatable."

"Well, don't you think that maybe that's because he is?"

"No, I think we can't beat him, because we can't see him being beaten."

David sat down, flustered at the conversation. "You're saying we can't beat him until we see him getting beaten?"

"Yes!" shouted Mitchell triumphantly.

David looked up almost piteously at his friend. "Mitchell, I don't want to pop your bubble or anything, but how does that help us?"

"We're going to beat him."

"Now I know you're crazy."

Mitchell slid his legs out in front of him and sat beside his friend. "We're not going to beat him by fighting him, we're going to beat him by humiliating him."

"Okay," came the cautious reply, "we can maybe do that, but when and how?"

"When is as soon as possible, which should be easy since he's already looking for us — the how is going to take some planning."

The boys spent the rest of the day plotting a way to get McNabb without getting themselves killed in the bargain. By lunch time they had hatched and discarded twenty-five different plans. Renewed with hot dogs, chips, and Kool-Aid, they finally came upon the one, single, sure-fire way to convince McNabb they weren't to be taken lightly.

The next time they went out they were fully prepared. It was almost disappointing when McNabb didn't show. They discussed it on the way home and rededicated themselves to their task. A week passed and still no McNabb.

Then on Friday it happened: McNabb returned. Again, Mitchell was hunting bugs and David scaling the rocks, but all was prepared for McNabb.

"Hey, baby! I think I hear your mommy calling you," was the cry that announced his arrival. It was punctuated by peals of laughter from the assembled McNabb followers. David looked down. There was McNabb, perched on David's bike, combing his shoulder-length hair, like he always did, and looking like king of the hill.

David double-checked to see that Mitchell had gone. "Okay, here goes nothing," he whispered to himself.

David stood up and yelled down. "Hey, get off my bike,

you overgrown rat!"

"Make me, you little sissy!" came the defiant reply.

At that taunt, David started throwing rocks as many and as quickly as he could. Some of McNabb's boys took refuge nearby, but McNabb fairly exploded with derision.

"Oh, you want to fight me now? My grandmother throws better and harder than you." He bellowed, tossing the bike aside and offering himself as a target. David took advantage of the situation and caught him square in the chest. McNabb's arrogance gave way to full-blown anger. The broad grin dissolved into a grim scowl.

"That's it Scharre, you've bought it this time." McNabb plowed through the creek. David continued to throw rocks at the charging opponent. This served to slow McNabb's progress. David kept close track of how fast and how well McNabb navigated the rocky hill. At the base, the gang came out of hiding cheering and whooping with approval.

Sensing it was time, David turned and worked his way up the rest of the hillside, McNabb moving faster behind and gaining since he no longer had to contend with the shower of rocks. Moving up the hill, David prayed under his breath. He broke the top of the hill and was positioning himself to sprint when McNabb's hand wrapped around his back foot. David fell on his face and heard McNabb's triumphant, "Got you! You little twerp." David twisted over on his back and as McNabb's head popped over the ridge, he caught it full in the face with his free foot. The effect was instantaneous. McNabb released his hold and slipped down the hill about four feet, scraping his hands on the way down.

David peered over the edge to see McNabb scrambling back up, then turned and ran for a small cluster of trees twenty or thirty feet beyond the ridge. As he feared and hoped, McNabb wasn't far behind. David bolted into the copse, McNabb not six feet behind him. David turned to see McNabb hit the edge of the trees and fall crashing to the ground. Stunned by the sudden impact with the earth, McNabb muttered obscenities as he picked himself up. He pushed himself half-way into a sitting position, then collapsed again; this time into unconsciousness.

Mitchell, with a large upraised stick, looked down at the now peaceful McNabb. "You know, looking at him like that, he doesn't look so big."

"Look at him later, he won't be out that long," hissed David.

"Okay, Okay — you know that big stick thing is good advice, I may use it again."

"Great, help me get him tied up, will you!" David's patience was a little on the short side. "I'm just glad you got up here in time. I kept thinking, what if he isn't there, then what am I going to do?"

"Well I got here, so there's nothing to worry about."

"Let's get this done and get out of here."

A few moments later their work done, Mitchell hobbled down the far path and David, after taking a moment to enjoy his handiwork, moved to the edge of the hill and waved at the McNabb gang. Delbert was the first to see that something was wrong.

"Come on, boys, let's get up there and see what done happened," he yelled, breaking across the creek and scrambling up the hill, the others close behind. David ran to catch up with Mitchell, stopping only to watch McNabb strain against his binding ropes and curse through the handkerchief that had been tied around his mouth.

Once back down the hill, Mitchell and David didn't wait for the response from above: they were too afraid to risk it. They did however hear a roar of laughter from the top of the hill as they rode away.

"One dragon down" said Mitchell.

"And none to go, I hope." added David.

Meanwhile, at the top of the hill, McNabb's former cronies were doubled over with laughter while he fumed and fought against the rope that held him to the tree. The boys had wanted to humiliate him, and they had succeeded. For there, on public display, was one Morton McNabb: bound, gagged, and stark naked to the sun and anyone else who happened to pass by.

For there, on public display, was one Morton McNabb. . . .

Dragon's Tears
Ginny Fleming

I love you.
There — I've said it.
Though by the very admission I've damned
myself to a smoldering eternity of exile. . . .
         I weep.

When I think of your smoky dark beauty,
both inside and out, I come close to realizing
the joy I will never hold to my heart. . . .
         I weep.

When I remember your deep jewel-blue eyes
and their whispered promise of pure love
freely given as you offer up your soul. . . .
         I weep.

When I recall shrouded memories of a long-gone
bliss spent in your strong embrace and the sacred
kisses we shared as lovers. . . .
         I weep.

When your precious voice comes to my ears
from across time, pledging eternal love with
your steamy parting breath. . . .
         I weep.

You vowed you would return to me, Love.
Yet, I look into your sapphire eyes and find
you have forgotten my face. . . .
And. . . .
         I weep.

The Dragon Incident
Elizabeth J. Gross

It is said all that glitters is not gold
The truth of every story is not always told.
They who think they know all will find . . . .
More times than not - it's a trick of the mind.

On a sunny summer day, Gregory Oliver came to
Lynchburg. He parked his Jeep Cherokee in front of the
Lynchburg Real Estate office, dropped a quarter in the
parking meter giving him an hour. He walked to the office
door, tried it, found it was locked. Shading his eyes with
both hands cupping his face, he peered through the glass
in the door. He tried knocking, but no one was there.

As he looked up and down Main Street of the small
southern town, he noted there were a couple of grocery
stores, post office, Woolworth's, a service station on the
corner, and the Town Hall directly across from the bank.
Two brown patrol cars were parked in front of the hall. The
car doors bore big stars that looked like badges with the
words "Lynch County Sheriff" written in a circle around
them. There was a spattering of undecipherable buildings,
the real estate office and the Dilly Dally Cafe next door.

He decided to go in the cafe — it looked like a local
hangout. More than likely, someone would know where the
agent was, how long he would be out and could tell him
something about the property.

He opened the cafe door; a cowbell over it clanked.
Five tables and chairs lined a wall and a counter with six bar
stools stuck out to the middle of the room. Two men sat at

the counter talking to the cook in a grease-splattered apron.

All three looked up when the cowbell clanked. Their conversation stopped while they studied the newcomer, trying to place him. He slid up on a bar stool and the man with the apron came over.

"What can I get ya'?" he asked.

"A hamburger, rare, dressed, a coke and maybe a little information," Greg said with a smile.

"Wellll, I can pretty much get ya' two of those things, but the third, I ain't shore of." He took a bun out of a Tastee Bread sack, put each end upside down on the grill, reached inside a refrigerator, took out a hamburger patty and slapped in on to cook.

Then he said, "What kinda information ya' needin'?"

"For starters, where's the real estate agent?"

The man laughed. "Thought it'd be a hard 'en. It's Wednesday afternoon. He and Doc Tate are playing golf."

The other two men at the counter snickered.

"Can't get sick or buy a house on Wednesday around here." One of the men offered.

"Can always get a burger here, though! Ain't that right, Clyde?" He nudged the other fellow with his elbow.

"Yeah, you can always get ptomaine on Wednesday afternoon," Clyde said holding his stomach.

"Shit! You ain't poisoned. It's a big fat hangover ya' got from all that drinking ya' done last night! Ain't that right, Dean?"

Dean and The Nudger guffawed. Greg grinned at the good natured kidding between the three men.

"Something else," Greg said, twisting around to face the two men. "Know anything about that property couple miles out on the highway that's for sale? Looks like a house burned there. Couple chimneys still standing." He saw Dean, the cook, stiffen and the other two look at each other.

No one said anything. Dean put tomato, lettuce and onion on top of the patty, lifted all with the spatula, laid it on one half of the bun. Smearing mayonnaise on the other half, he mashed it all down and put it on the counter in front of Greg. Then he asked:

"Why ya' wantin' to know? Not aiming to buy it, are ya'?"

"Thought I might. Anything wrong with the property?"

"Wellll, it ain't exactly prime real estate, if ya' ask me!" The Nudger said. "Wouldn't touch it with a ten-foot pole!"

Swallowing a bite, Greg asked, "Could I ask why?"

Dean placed Greg's coke on the counter. It was one of those little green bottles, foaming with tiny shards of ice on top.

"Been up for sale for a while. No lookers, well, maybe a few, but no takers," Dean said.

"Looks like a piece of good property, " Greg offered.

"Looks good, okay, but the hard facts is, it ain't!"

"Why's that?"

"Wellll," said Nudger, twirling an ash tray on the counter. "There was that dragon incident!"

"Shit-fire, Charlie! My folks ain't ever gonna sell it if you tell people that!" Clyde wailed.

"Well, it's the truth, ain't it?" demanded Charlie.

"Yeah, well, maybe the truth, but telling the truth won't sell it! Hell!" Clyde muttered.

"Welll," Charlie drawled, "anybody gonna buy it, needs to know, I'm thinkin'."

"What IS the truth?" Greg asked.

Dean sighed, leaned on the counter and said "I'll tell it! Clyde there," he said pointing, "is Clyde Koons. His family's lived here a long time. His dad grew up in that house out there. His aunt Molly Koons lived on there by herself long after their ma and pa died. She was always a little different. She was an old maid and also a loner. Kids in this town used to go out there and torment her. Scare her a lot, rake sticks against her house, set little fires on her property and run. Things like that. She'd get mad, yell and scream at 'em. Then, she took to shootin' a BB gun at 'em. Things kinda escalated." He straightened up, turned a little, stared out the window and said "Things got bad . . . really bad after that. Then came that awful day four years ago". . . .

⁂

Molly snatched the tabloid from the rack, pitched her groceries on the checkout belt and began to read the first paragraph.

"You want that *Globe*?"

"What?"

"I said you want that magazine? The manager don't like people reading and not buying."

"I want it and I'm buying it! Satisfied?"

The cashier shrugged and rang up the magazine.

She hurried toward home; the top part of her torso bent forward and her short, fat legs not quite keeping up.

She jay-walked twice, oblivious to nearly being hit by a pick-up truck. The driver yelled, "Get out of the way you damn crazy woman!" He blew his horn, but it didn't penetrate because her mind was on what happened the day before. That was when she had first seen the trail in her yard. It looked nearly identical to *The Globe's* tracks. The

only difference — there were no feet tracks.

In her kitchen, she dropped the sack on the table, ignorant of the fact that she broke the eggs. She quickly grabbed *The Globe* and retreated to the living room couch, settled in and began to read.

In big letters *The Globe* proclaimed:

"WOMAN EATEN BY DRAGON!"

The story went on to say:

A Florida woman was eaten last week by what authorities believe was a fire-breathing dragon. Bones of Agnes Jones were found under a willow tree, gnawed and charred. Authorities believe the creature probably came out of the Everglades."It had to be a carnivorous animal of tremendous size", said Sheriff Glen Martin, of Little Grove, Florida. "The teeth left huge gouges in the bones. See the tracks made by the feet?" he asked. "They are larger than a grizzly bear's and the trail of the tail measures four inches across. It appears we are discussing a huge animal. Probably taller than the grizzly and weighing at least as much. I'd say we've got our work cut out for us!"

***

Molly studied the pictures of the woman's charred bones. The caption under the gruesome photograph stated they were incinerated at an extremely high temperature, without any chemical traces.

She leaned back on the couch, dropping the tabloid

in her lap.

"Oh my!" she said, gripping her hand across her mouth. "I've got a dragon! Just like that Florida woman!"

At that moment there was a loud slap against the side of the house right behind her back. She sprang up screaming, *The Globe's* pages falling to the floor. Then there was the scraping noise of sticks dragging along the side of the house.

She bolted to the window, raised it and shouted "Get away! Get away, you terrible little monsters!"

The three boys laughed and ran to the field behind the house, thumbing their noses at her chanting, "Nah-nah-nah!"

Molly ran to the backdoor, grabbed the BB gun that was leaning against the wall, rushed out the door, which slammed shut behind her. She aimed the gun toward the boys and shot several BBs. Still laughing, the hoodlums ran across the field. She yelled, shook her fist and went back in the house.

Later in the day, she smelled smoke. Stepping out on her front porch she saw one end of it was on fire. She ran to the water faucet, turned it on, dragged the hose around to the front of the house and doused the fire. Then she saw the tracks coming from underneath the porch going down to the willow tree. The dragon had set fire to her porch!

"Oh, my goodness!" She moaned. "It's under the willow!" She turned and ran back in the house. She jerked open a closet door, pulled down a twelve-gauge double-barreled shotgun. "This'll take more than a BB gun," she muttered, putting a shell into each barrel. She dropped two more in her apron pocket for good measure, and trotted back to the front porch. The fire had caught again and was licking the roof.

***

Sheriff James Dotson was eating lunch at his desk when the dispatcher, Lynn Eden, took a call from Danny Shields. Lynn tapped on the door, stuck her head in and said," Jimmy, I hate to bother you, but this is a pretty good 'un. You know Danny Shields, that young boy what owns that big ol' snake? Well, he just called to say it has gotten out of its cage and is outside somewheres. Says he needs help with trapping it. You want me to radio Tom to go on over there?"

"Nah," said Jimmy, wiping his mouth with a napkin, "he's scared shitless of a snake, any size, much less a boa constrictor. He ain't gonna be much help there."

Standing up, he said, "I'll run on over there, myself." Putting on his hat and heading out the door, he said, "Might be awhile at this. That damn snake'll have a good place to hide if it gets in that thicket between the Shield's and that Koons woman's. She's let that place grow up like a jungle."

He closed the door, went to his patrol car and headed East out Highway 64.

***

Molly crept toward the tree, holding the shotgun straight out in front of her face, sighting down the barrel. Because of the massive drooping branches of the willow, she couldn't see under it. When she was maybe within a foot of it she heard a noise coming from behind the thicket of branches. She fired the right barrel.

When the shot went under the willow, it hit Tommy Jordan, tearing off his right ear, taking the side of his face, eye, cheek, and jawbones. That same blast of the gun cut the boa constrictor in half. What was left of the reptile hung down the side of the tree. A partially-digested rabbit dangled from the twitching snake's severed belly.

Molly, hearing a noise from the other side of the tree, fired the left barrel. The shot tore through the branches, taking the left arm and shoulder of Joshua Smith and the center of little Benny Owens' chest, killing him instantly.

At that precise moment, Sheriff Dotson and Danny Shields were tromping around in the thicket between the Sheilds' and Koons' property. They heard the two gun blasts and the screaming and howling. Beating their way back through the briars and brambles, the Sheriff yelled at Danny, "Get in your house and stay there!" Jimmy Dotson pulled his gun from his holster as he ran.

Coming up the Koons' driveway, he saw the porch was on fire and Molly Koons standing by the willow tree reloading the shotgun.

"Stop!" he screamed. "Stop!".

Molly paused between loading the shotgun barrels and gaped at the Sheriff as he ran towards her.

"Hold it, Molly, and put down that gun! Now!" He stopped, legs spread apart, in the middle of the driveway. "Drop it, Molly, or I'll shoot! Just lay it down, real easy!"

Molly stooped and laid the gun on the ground.

"What in hell is going on?" he yelled. "What's under there?" he asked, jerking his head towards the willow.

"It's a dragon! I shot it twice, and it's still not dead! You hear it?"

Sheriff Dotson eased sideways towards the tree, keeping his eyes on Molly. "Move away from that gun, Molly! Go on over by that maple and sit down! Now!" She inched over towards the maple tree.

Molly crept toward the tree, holding the shotgun
straight out in front of her face

"Go on! Go on! If you so much as look at that gun, I'll shoot you! You hear me?"

Molly nodded, went to the maple and sat down on the ground.

The Sheriff crept to the willow, his gun held out in front of him. He bent down, parted the tree branches, said, "Lord God A'Mighty!" and puked.

❋

"Wellll," Dean continued, "Little Timmy Jordan's had extensive surgery to repair his face, and still has a lot of operations to go, not even talking about what's going on in his head. Benny Owens was killed right out, with Joshua Smith dying a couple days later. Old Molly, wellll, she's up at Our Lady Of Sorrow's Hospital. She'll be there the rest of her life. Crazy as a bat. Rants and raves all the time."

When Dean finished his story, no one spoke for awhile. He cleared away Greg's empty plate and coke bottle.

"Wellll, ya' still think ya' might be interested in the Koons' place?" Dean asked.

"Not much."

"Yeah, wellll, it does kinda put a slant on it, don't it?"

"Sure does."

"If ya' still interested in living around here, and ya' like us," Dean grinned, "Ya' could come by the real estate office tomorrow. There's the Perry place down that a'ways," Dean pointed to the far wall, "It's a nice place. No dragons I heard of."

Greg laughed. "Yeah, I think I'll do that." He stood up, gave Dean a ten dollar bill. Dean punched the cash register, counted out change and gave it to Greg.

"I sure would like to know what happened to that dragon in the Florida Everglades!" Clyde chuckled.

"Hell, boy, an alligator big as Godzilla crawled outta there and swallowed that damn dragon whole!" Charlie hooted.

"SHIIIT!"

Greg opened the door.

"Hey, reckon whatever happened to that alligator?" Clyde asked.

Dean and Charlie roared. Greg laughed and shut the door.

His Jeep Cherokee had a parking ticket on it.

Sanctum Ad Terminus

Jeannine Baumgartle

It's spring.
I sweep away at my
dustless hearth,
wishing the buds
from the hawthorns
and the lark's regress
to a southern shore.
My shining one,
my soul blossom,
stands before the window
combing her hair gold.
She must go
with the rest,
find passage through
those dark hills
where the dragon
blocks entry.
No one can hide.
The dragon knows when
maidens come of age
and youths
lean toward adventure,
lures them
with a glimpse of
sapphire horizon
beyond which understanding
is to be found,
the secret of dust,
and one morning
they all must go,
armed with nothing
but a name
and their own wits.
Who will make it,
who will not.
We parents watch
from our doorways,
wring our hands
in silence,
then return
to the cottage
that will never
be the same.

The Jade Dragon

T. Lee Harris

Some mornings you're better off to stay in bed. Last Wednesday was like that — only I couldn't. It was the second Wednesday of the month and that meant the regular meeting with Steadfast Investigations and Security Inc.'s regional manager. The guy's name was O'Malley, but he was a dead ringer for Boris Yeltsin and he didn't like me much. Feeling was mutual.

The review didn't go well. But then again, in the eight months since I quit the FBI and opened the Louisville branch of Steadfast, few of them had. Louisville was a closemouthed town that didn't usually seek an outside source for a solution to its private problems.

If the day started badly, nothing happened during its course to lift it to more pleasant territory. No new clients, and one we already had told us if we couldn't come up with something better on his wife than night classes at Bellarmine, to take a hike. Even the weather was oppressive — one of those gray days that seem to suck light into them. There wasn't any work to do, but I was still the last to leave and, as I locked up the office, the clouds that had been threatening all day made good on it and cut loose with a cold drizzle. The prospect of battling my cat for a microwaved Le Menu in my apartment lost what little charm it had in the face of the rain, so I veered away from the parking lot and headed around the corner to my favorite Chinese place.

The aromas seeping out of the Jade Dragon started working on me before I could even see the sign over the door. That was going some: the sign was a neon masterpiece depicting a twisting Chinese dragon in vivid red, blue and green. Tonight, the neon beacon painted splashes of color over the wet pavement as I jogged through the rain toward the good smells.

The place was packed with dragons, most of them plastic, except for the one in the glass case behind the cash register. That was one venerable worm. Genuine white jade, a family treasure for better than 600 years, and the piece itself was thought to be much older than that. According to Harvey Leong, Prop., it was a sky dragon. Didn't mean much to me, but beaucoup to Harve. I asked once why the thing wasn't in a bank vault or on loan to a nice, safe museum and was told the dragon had to preside over the family doings it was tradition. Tradition, maybe, but not good security. I guess the best protection was that

no one believed anything so valuable would be on such prominent display — especially in a hole-in-the-wall eatery like the one bearing its name.

As I stepped in, the dragons and Harve were the only visible occupants of the restaurant. Telltale pot-banging penetrated the swinging steel door, announcing the presence of Pam Leong, Mrs. Prop. in the kitchen. Harve looked as happy as I felt as he called:

"Evenin', Dallas. Got some of that General Tso chicken with them little chunks of zucchini tonight. Real spicy, the way you like it. Getcha some?"

It was weird hearing a Kentucky drawl coming out of a guy who looked like supporting cast for The Last Son of Heaven, but that was Harve right down to the ground. He was third generation Louisvillian on account of his great grandparents followed the railroads from the West coast as far as Louisville, then settled in. They swore blue that it was because the Ohio River valley looked like a great place to raise a family. Pam, always the cynic, suspects it was simply where the money ran out. Pam's childhood in Viet Nam left her with a lot of doubts about human nature. Coming home with a gem of a GI husband like Harve only went a little way to smooth those over.

I ordered the chicken and sat in the corner booth to lick my wounds when all of a sudden a bottle of Ki-rin beer dropped onto the table and Harve dropped into the seat opposite me.

"You look like you could use this." He grimaced and took a pull at his own, saying:

"You ain't alone. Cops busted my nephew today, said he was dealin' at school. Stupid kid."

"Geez. This is his third bust, isn't it? That's bad news."

"You don't know the half of it! It ain't enough we're short handed on account of Lonnie gettin' busted, but his mom — my sister, she gets all hysterical and goes home early. Wife's been coverin' the kitchen solo all day. Then to top it off, we get an order for the special seafood soup, and when I was in the freezer getting the squid, . . . here!"

Something whacked my knee under the table, and puzzled, I took the thing out of Harve's hands before he could dislocate my patella. The packet wasn't very large, but solid and wrapped in plastic. Honoring Harve's caution, I glanced at it below the table edge, and just about knocked the beer over shoving it back whence it came.

"Holy shit, Harve, that's crack! Turn it over to the police."

"I know what it is, and I can't give it to the cops. Lonnie may be a dumbass, but he's family. I if they add this amount of shit to what he had on him, it'll go real bad for him. Kill his mom for sure. Bad enough they got him sellin' to an undercover cop, but with this . . . ? Lucky he wasn't sellin' out of the restaurant, or maybe me and Pam'd be in the slammer, too."

"So turn it over to Levitz! He's a cop and you know him; he's in here all the time!"

"No can do. Last thing I want is to have the cops all over my place. Jeezus! I don't even wanna think what the Board of Health would say. But you, you're not so official . . . ."

"So what am I supposed to do? I was FBI, not DEA."

"You know people — you know how things work. Get

rid of it for me, huh, Dallas?"

"Wha-a-a-t?"

"Dump it in the river. Somethin'. Anything! I can't, the cops might be watchin' me and this place right now."

"That's destruction of evidence and obstruction of an ongoing police investigation."

"Oh, man! Don't go all Fed on me! I'm worried, God knows who that lamebrained kid told about his stash. I need help, and you're the only guy I know t'ask. Believe me, I'm desperate enough to light incense sticks in front of the dragon like my Pop useta."

"You lost me there, Harve."

"The sky dragon." He jerked his thumb toward the translucent white carving in the case behind the counter, and continued:

"Him. I told you he's been in the family for centuries, but I didn't tell you the legend. My ancestors believed he was a real dragon or a dragon-spirit trapped in jade. Any of the Leong clan is threatened, the dragon is supposed to come to their rescue or something like that. Truth t'tell, I never listened when my Granpa was tellin' his stories about the old days. I could really use somethin' like that, though — a guardian spirit.

"Nice story. When you get around to that incense, light one up for me, huh?"

"Oh yeah. Today was O'Malley day, wasn't it."

Outside the storm got down to serious business. Lightning flashed and the overhead lights flickered in sympathy. Harve swivelled to glare out at the rain:

"Damn. As if things wasn't dead enough, this rain's gonna keep 'em away in droves. Might just close up early and head home."

※※※

When the three kids came in, I was downing the last of my hot tea and staring at the innocuous white bag that held my leftover chicken, crab rangoon, and the styrofoam clamshell containing the drugs. I still hadn't decided what to do with it, and was kicking myself for letting Harve talk me into taking it off the premises.

The kids were jumpy and Harve didn't look real pleased to see them. He folded the newspaper he was reading and slipped it under the counter saying:

"If you guys are lookin' for dinner, we're just about to close, and if you're lookin' for Lonnie, he ain't here. In case you didn't hear, he got busted today."

Since it was still only the two of us in front, they got braver. Harve is an older guy a little on the heavy side, and I'm wiry, but not what you'd call impressive by any stretch of the imagination. They fanned out and got down to business. The largest one stood in front of Harve and demanded:

"You know why we're here, old man. We want Lonnie's stash. Just hand it over and no one hasta get hurt."

Harve protested that he didn't know what they were talking about but I have to confess, even if I hadn't known he was lying, I wouldn't have believed him either. Harve was a rotten liar. The kid hassling him gave him a shove that sent him straight into the case containing the sky dragon. The case probably made a helluva crash when it broke, but you couldn't prove it by me. At the instant it hit the floor, there was the mother of all thundercracks as lightning struck somewhere close. The lights flickered wildly, then went out for good. I took advantage of the confusion by diving for the floor, sweeping the bag off the table as I went. I crouched in the shelter of the booth, taking my bearings, and stopped in amazement when I found the cash register. The storm was strobing irregularly now, sending intermittent flashes of blue light into the dining area. The psychedelic light show must have been playing with my mind, but I swear that for just an instant, the jade dragon was glowing faintly. Then thunder crashed again and I had other things on my mind.

The kid who decked Harve sang out:

"I think I know where to look, you guys take care of things out here."

The others grunted agreement and started sidling around looking for me. I didn't feel like being helpful, so I moved out. Mindful of the broken glass, I crawled commando style to the counter and slid behind it. There hadn't been so much as a peep from Harve since he went down and I was worried. I also thought maybe I could reach the phone to dial 911. It was good news, bad news: Harve was alive, but the phone wasn't. I froze, listening. Other than the storm and a strange slithering sound, there was nothing. I hadn't heard a thing from the kitchen since the blackout, either. I hoped that was a good thing.

Suddenly one of the kids let out a shriek and fell into some tables with a crash punctuated by a small explosion and muzzle flash. Panicked scrabbling and swearing followed. Just to my right, his pal snapped:

"Shit! Just who you tryin' to shoot, Butthead?"

"I . . . I stepped on somethin' maybe a rat . . . I dropped my gun."

The other turned away muttering:

"Good. It's safer that way."

Great. Nervous punks with guns. The only good thing about it was that if Pam was unaware of the goings-on in the front, she damn well knew now. I hoped she'd made it out the back door and was legging it for help. With Pam you never knew. I pulled my own weapon and made for the far end of the counter, away from the voice.

There was a clatter from the kitchen, but before I could think about it much, the kid to my right started squalling like his friend had earlier.

"Goddamn, it is a rat! Owwww! Shit! It bit me!"

From the racket, I figured he must've fallen into the carts Pam sorted the flatware and glasses on. He was flailing around in a way that was horrible to hear, screaming about being eaten alive.

I didn't know what was chewing on the kid, and frankly didn't care. With all the noise he was making, I figured this was my best bet to make a beeline for the police. I hated leaving Harve in the hands of these creeps, but he was still out cold; there was no way to carry him out unnoticed. I oozed out from behind the cash register, only to find myself nose to nose with the kid looking for his dropped pistol. His fear was pungent. As the lightning flashed again he saw I had a weapon of my own. He tried to grapple it. I let him, then pressed the trigger. He jerked, dropping to the floor, alive, but a prisoner in his own body. As long as you're on the right end of the things, stun guns are wonderful inventions.

❄✳❄

Soon after that the lights and phone came back on line. With his friend in front wearing my cuffs and still woozy,

the kid with the rat fixation gave up without a fight. I can't take credit for that, though. If my first sight when the lights came on was Pam Leong brandishing a cast-iron tea kettle in my face, I'd have surrendered, too.

The guy in the kitchen was lucky the kettle only grazed him or it would have fractured his skull like an eggshell. He was still out and, all in all, that worked out for the best. I sent Pam to the front to call the cops and, once she was gone, I slid the bag of crack into the kid's jacket. We lucked out more when Levitz answered the call as Officer In Charge.

The screamer kept swearing the joint was rat-infested and that one attacked him in the dark. Sure enough, when the medics treated him, he was covered with scratches that had shredded his jeans and there were several tiny bitemarks on him. Trouble was, they didn't look like any rodent bite I'd ever seen.

Harve and I looked at each other, then over at the dragon. It was lying atop the remains of its case behind the counter, but its color seemed slightly deeper than before; like scudding clouds in the sunshine, and . . . this sounds crazy, but there was a pinkish tint around its grinning muzzle that I didn't remember seeing before.

The cops left with the kids and the drugs in custody. Levitz paused at the door, and warned:

"You better get an exterminator in here first thing tomorrow, Harve, or the Heath Inspectors will be all over you about this."

Harve agreed:

"You bet!" As the door closed behind the officers, Harve added:

"It'll be the second call I make."

I grinned:

"Who's the first, Harve, the insurance company or your lawyer?"

"Neither. I'm callin' the company that makes those display cases."

I followed his gaze to the statue now resting on the counter, and nodded:

"You might want to lay in some incense, too."

The Transformation
Marian Allen

Yesterday

I was a tender maid,
muscles firm, eyes bright.
Today
my skin is wrinkled leather
covered with rough white scales.
I make noise walking;
my body large, unwieldy.

And do I guard my treasure?
Hoard it with bitter jealousy,
gloating, pinning it firmly
beneath my reddened claws?
I do.

"I do."
We spoke those words
of brightest power and the spell
began. The decades of enchantment
ended when the life of the enchanter
ended.
See what I have become.

And what is left but treasure?
Coin, jewels, artifacts, remembrances
still warm from the enthrallment,

charming my heart to holocaust,
burning my eyes with salt.

Dim are the eyes of my reflection,
smoke-dim from the flame
that burns inside,
        consuming me
                as once the flame consumed
the tender maid.

The Hired Hand

Joy Kirchgessner

Hannah propped herself on her knees in the middle of her bed and peered out the window into the darkness. Jovial male voices commingling with the jingle of harness chains announced the arrival of team and wagon. As it drew near the barn, the only illumination was a lantern hanging from the buckboard's side.

"We'll put the horses away and then you can make your quarters in the barn. There's a cot in the tack room."

Hannah recognized her stepfather's inebriated voice, smelled the stench of his whiskey-laden breath in her imagination, but another man was with him and this man was staying the night.

She strained to see beyond the lantern's soft glow as it came off its perch on the wagon. Seemingly by itself — though she knew it was by someone's hand — the light hovered first near one horse, then the other like some giant firefly.

"I'll put the horses away, boss. You go on in and get some sleep," suggested the stranger.

Despite the fact that she couldn't make him out, she knew her stepfather was headed for the house. The squeaky hinges of the kitchen door betrayed his entrance. He stumbled over something solid that scooted across the wooden floor.

"Son of a . . . ," he growled in a half finished curse.

She traced him through the house by the sound of his

footsteps and held her breath as he hesitated at the bottom of the staircase. With any luck he would sleep downstairs; sometimes he came up to Momma's room and made her cry--like the night before when he gave her a black eye. Momma had so far protected her from his physical abuse. Ron was always ill-tempered and growing worse. Hannah's friends at school had told her their parents talked about him. "He spends time at the local bar with lowbred women and brags that he'd just up and leave one day to go further west to seek his fortune in the gold mines." Her friends didn't know the half of it.

Footsteps again . . . he passed on by.

She let out a sigh of relief and returned her attention to the bobbing lantern. It was in the barn now; she could see it shining between the slats. When the light finally went out she lay back down musing over the newcomer until she nodded off.

She awoke the next morning to the comforting smells of breakfast which filled the house: bacon frying, coffee, and hot bread. It was enough incentive to get going if only by the will of an empty stomach. She quickly dressed and trotted downstairs to help in the kitchen.

"Good morning sweetheart. Help momma set the table," greeted a tender voice.

"Momma, there's a man sleeping in the barn."

"I know honey, Ron hired a fellow to help with the farm. The neighbors don't seem to have the time anymore. I can't blame them; he doesn't return the favor," she said looking out the window. "Here comes Ron and the man now."

The screen door opened; in walked Hannah's stepfather

followed by a tall muscular man with wavy auburn hair and skin the color of copper from working long hours in the sun. He politely introduced himself as George Sonders — Ron made little effort at these formalities especially where his family was concerned.

Smiling timidly her mother answered, "Miriam . . . my name is. . .

"That's my wife." Ron cut in. "Come on in, George, and pull up a chair."

Hannah took a seat across the table from their guest.

"Well now, who might we have here?" asked George.

Before Hannah could answer Ron redirected the conversation towards the day's work.

Miriam brought the biscuits over and proceeded to sit but stopped at the sound of Ron slowly tapping his fork on the table top. This was his way of indicating she had forgotten something. She looked the table over in this twisted guessing game then brought the butter and sat down.

When a lull in the conversation ensued George inquired (referring to the bruised flesh around her eye), "If you don't mind me saying so, ma'am, that's quite a nasty shiner you've got there."

Hannah, feeling a great secret was about to be exposed, looked at her mother anticipating her reply. She listened as Miriam lied about how a piece of kindling flew up and hit her as she tried to chop it small enough to fit in the stove. Hannah watched George to see if he would swallow that one.

"I can chop the wood for you, ma'am," offered George.

"She can do that for herself, that's her job and she

doesn't mind, do you Miriam?" Ron hissed. "Besides, it's high time we get started with the farm work."

George thanked Miriam and excusing himself, went out the door.

Ron stayed behind for a few minutes with some instructions. Emphasizing each word by pointing his finger at them he said, "I don't want that man up around this house for any reason other than meals. Do we all understand each other." It was a statement not a question, with that he marched out.

A week went by and Miriam never had to chop a stick of kindling. Mysteriously, there was always a pile ready for the day's cooking requirements. Not one or the other ever mentioned this to Ron.

It was now Sunday — a day of rest for most. Hannah always walked to the river. A short distance really, but it seemed like a big adventure through field and woods for a nine year old girl. She pretended she was a royal member of the court in the flower covered kingdom of the birds and deer. When she reached the riverside she stooped down and tried to sneak up on a frog — which saw her first and jumped in with a splash. She picked up a stone and to her delight skipped it three times across the top of the water.

"Very good, Ronette," came a voice that gave her a start.

It was George. He was sitting in the shade up against the trunk of a very large sycamore tree whittling on a small piece of wood.

"What did you call me?" She asked as she slowly walked toward him.

"You're the smallest member of Ron's family, so I called

you Ronette. The ette means small."

"You know my name is Hannah and besides, Ron is not my real father."

"Please forgive me . . . Hannah . . . I did not intend to offend."

"What are you making?" she asked as she leaned over to get a better look.

"A winged denizen of the trees" He held out a tiny carving of a bird no bigger than a finch.

"Now, watch this." He cupped the carving in his calloused hands, hiding it for a moment, and then he opened them. A living bird was in his palm; it hopped once using George's fingers as a vaulting board and flew off into the forest.

"How did you do that?" she nearly whispered.

"It's magic. I've carved something for you too . . . if you'd like." He held out a roughly oval shaped pendant suspended from a cotton string for a necklace. "It's a dragon." He traced the curves with his finger. "Dragons are guardians. If you wear it, it will keep you from harm."

She put it around her neck and they sat and chatted for a while then started for home, picking daisies for her mother along the way at Hannah's suggestion. When they arrived home she delivered the bouquet to her mother who was sweeping the porch. George came along at Hannah's insistence — she had forgotten Ron's warning.

"Oooh, how pretty," Miriam praised and she kissed her on the check.

"George is going to teach me how to whittle," she boasted. "Look what he made for me." She held the pendant up for her mother to see.

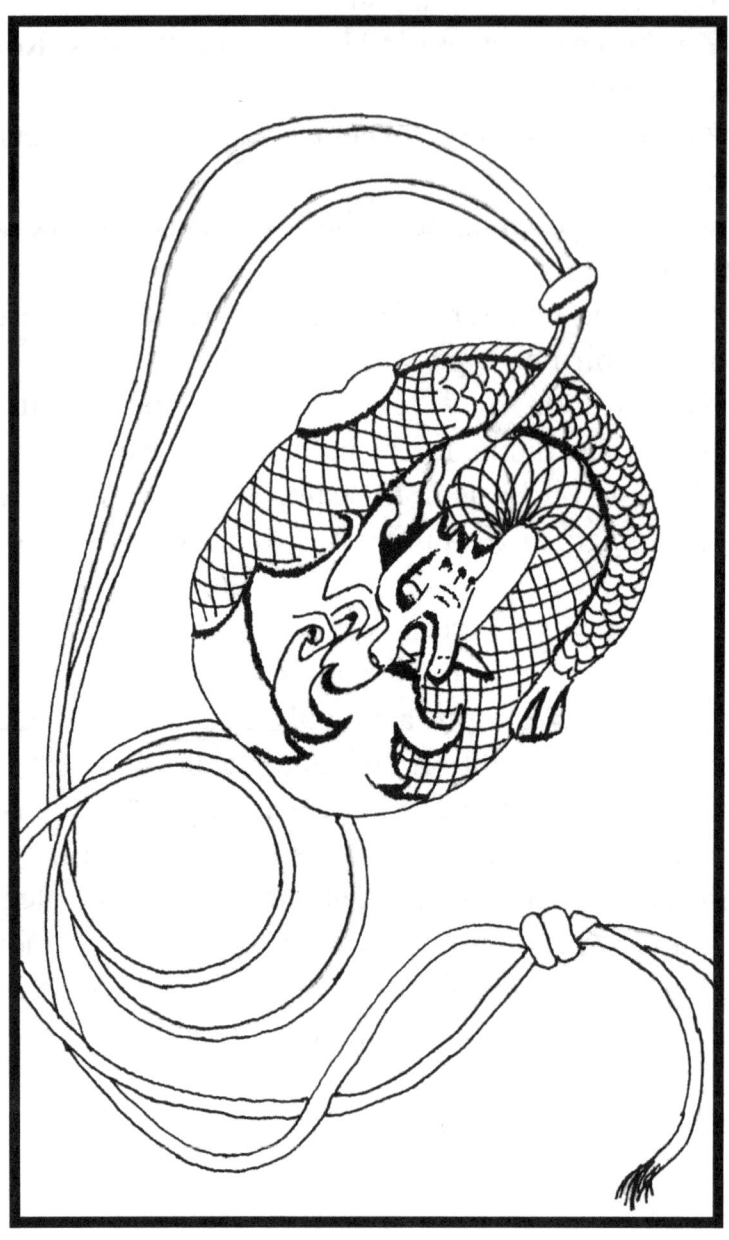

... a roughly oval shaped pendant suspended from
a cotton string for a necklace.

"That's very nice," Miriam barely looked at the trinket. She was keeping an eye out for Ron. "Run along now . . . and don't be late for supper."

"We'll just be outside the barn, ma'am," said George as Hannah took him by the hand and pulled him along.

They were passing an open shed just a few hundred yards from the house when something hit George so hard from behind that he collapsed on the ground. Ron loomed over George's motionless body gripping a shovel.

"That's for doing my wife favors behind my back. I'll be putting those flowers on both your graves," he ranted through clenched teeth.

Hannah was still within reach, petrified with horror. Never dropping his club, Ron grabbed her arm and squeezed so tightly she thought it was going to break. "You've probably all been laughing behind my back. I'll teach you a lesson you'll never forget."

"You're hurting me! You're hurting me!" she wailed. "Mamaaaa!

Miriam had already heard and came running. She pulled at Ron's arm with all her might. "Let her go, damn you!"

He did and turned his rage towards Miriam. She slowly backed away with Ron following.

"You should be afraid, you lousy whore."

Hannah knelt down sobbing beside George, trying to rouse him. He came to but couldn't do more than turn his head in her direction and say, "Clasp your hands around your pendant tightly; whatever happens don't let go."

She interlocked her fingers about the pendant as if in prayer and looked into George's eyes for reassurance.

"Have faith in yourself," George encouraged.

She watched her hands as a thick mist leaked between her fingers like steam from a tea kettle only instead of being hot it made her hands tingle. As the mist enveloped her the tingling spread down her spine giving every nerve an unearthly energy and causing her to close her eyes for a second. She opened her eyes and one small tear flowed down her cheek. The mist twirled growing bigger and upward as if she were in the eye of a tornado. Then it slowed to a stop, took form and uncoiled. The dragon! It drew it's head and neck upward and back like stretching from a long sleep.

Ron had his back to the creature, shovel raised, ready to strike Miriam. She with her head turned eyes closed and arms in front of her face ready to defend herself as best she could from the blow. At that moment the dragon, mouth open, came down upon Ron and with one jerking motion swallowed him whole. Then. as quickly as it had formed it shrank back to the pendant. No one moved for a moment, like animals that have been caged all their lives and suddenly someone opens the door.

Hannah ran to her mother. She wasn't quite sure what had happened or if what had happened was real or some half-dream. They went over to help George who was on his hands and knees attempting to get up off the ground.

*****

Two weeks went by and each day Miriam feared that Ron might reappear. She decided that they should return to her parents home in Boston. Though no one ever spoke of the phenomenon, Hannah knew in her heart that their worst days were over.

George volunteered to stay at the farm until arrangements

could be made to sell it. He promised them he would be fine. He also carved Hannah a new pendant — throwing the other one in the river. This pendant had a bird on it. He called it a "Phoenix"; said that it was more fitting now. Hannah would have to look that word up when she reached Boston.

The Dragon's Lair
Glenda Mills

Ellen pulled up slowly, stopping her car beside the small, white wooden booth, a rickety old sentry standing guard at the entrance to the Monroe County Fairgrounds. She rolled her window down, the oppressive July heat slamming her in the face. She handed five dollars to an elderly woman who stood under the shade of the building fanning herself with a square poster board fan stapled to a flat wooden stick, "Curtis for City Council" printed in large glaring red letters.

She made her way down the gravel road toward the grassy area designated as row two. Ellen was thankful for one thing: It hadn't rained in over a week and, as a result, the long hot summer days had baked the ground as hard as asphalt. Back when she was a little girl, she could remember tractors dragging out car after car, mired down in the. . . .

"Hey, Mom, can I get some cotton candy, please?"

The "please" was a high drawn-out squeal. Ellen closed her eyes for a moment, fighting off the headache that was lingering at each temple, waiting for the heat and the noise to beckon it forth in full intensity.

Evan had already undone his seat belt and was standing with his head stuck between the front bucket seats where the view was better. He reminded her of a kiddie commando in his camouflage T-shirt and flat-top haircut. His brown eyes sparkled with the excitement of the upcoming battle where, armed with a handful of tickets, a pocketful of change, and a heart full of youth, he would pillage, plunder and conquer — at least until Mom said he had to go home. The thought of following him into battle only heightened the exhaustion Ellen had been fighting for days.

Evan didn't seem to notice her long, deep sigh. He was already opening his car door, ramming it into the door of the car beside them in his haste. Ellen inspected the damage. A small chip of paint was missing, nothing anyone would notice. She looked up from the car to find her son already at the end of the row and turning for the main gate.

"Evan Brent Marshall, stop! Quit that running and wait for me!" Ellen had to yell to get his attention, causing the throbbing in her temples to intensify once again.

Evan slowed to a trot. Realizing her plight, she decided to catch up before her son became a large hood ornament on someone's car and bolted after him, grabbing him by the collar of his T-shirt somewhere between row one and the main gate.

"I told you not to run," she scolded between quick short breaths.

"I wasn't running. I was walking fast."

Ellen rolled her eyes. If nothing else, at least the kid had a chance at a political career.

"Whatever. Just make sure not to do any fast walking once we're inside the fairgrounds."

"Sure thing, Mom." Evan turned toward her with an angelic smile and devilment dancing in his eyes.

The first stop after entering the main gate was the concession stand. Evan got his cotton candy, a large blue Q-tip which he stopped momentarily to admire before burying his face ear-deep into its sugary softness. Ellen settled for a shriveled hot dog on a soggy bun, admitting to herself that somehow a hot dog that cost a buck fifty at the fairgrounds really did taste better than the ones you made at home. The mother in her cringed at the very thought.

"Can we go on some rides now, please?" Two sticky hands reached up, shaking her arm, causing her to spill Big Red down her white tank top and denim shorts.

"Sorry, Mom." She stared down at the back of his head. He was watching the ground, making circles in the dust with his tennis shoes.

"All I've got to say, young man, is that it's a good thing tie-dye is back in style. Otherwise, you would be in a world of hurt. Now, how about getting some tickets?"

Evan bolted off toward the ferris wheel in search of a ticket booth. By the time Ellen caught up with him, he was hopping impatiently from foot to foot beside a white stand with the word "tickets" flashing above it in yellow lights.

"Mom, over here. I found it."

The headache that had been threatening was now firmly established. Ellen closed her eyes for a moment, hoping the darkness would help. She wanted to go home and lie down, but home was hundreds of miles from the Monroe County Fairgrounds. For the past two weeks, she had spent every available minute at the hospital, sitting at her mother's bedside, watching her die little by little. Evan had been cooped up at his aunt's house, surrounded by people he knew only as signatures on Christmas cards. They both needed a break, and the fair had seemed a good opportunity to take their minds off things for awhile. At least it was working for Evan.

"Mom, hey Mom." The hopping had turned into an all-out dance.

"I'm coming. Settle down, for Pete's sake. The rides aren't going anywhere."

She purchased a book of tickets and headed into the midway, struggling to keep up with Evan as he darted in and out of the crowd at a seemingly impossible pace. He rounded the corner between the carousel and the Tilt-O-Whirl and stopped. He just stood there, looking straight ahead. As Ellen made her way toward him, she saw it, the object of her son's awe, and she stopped too.

In front of them was a huge, green dragon; its metallic skin glared and glistened in the sun's rays. The beast had piercing red eyes and orange and red flames shooting from its mouth. Its serpentine tail lay coiled around its dagger claws. Within its belly, people writhed in black cars, jerked and twisted first one way then another at a speed that blurred their faces as they raced past. Their screams mixed with the electronic growls and roars of the dragon, giving it a surreal dimension that sent a shiver down Ellen's sweaty neck. She hadn't thought about The Dragon's Lair in years.

✻✻✻

She had been no older than Evan the first year the green beast arrived at the fair. Her reaction had also been one of amazement. She thought it was the neatest ride in the whole world, and she begged her mother to let her go on it.

"Certainly not. You are much too young for a ride like that. When you get older, we'll discuss it."

The next year, Ellen had implored her mother once again, pointing out that she was a whole year older and at least an inch taller than the previous year. Her mother said no, because she had just eaten two hot dogs, a carton of

Mom, can I ride it, please? Its totally awesome.

popcorn, and cotton candy, washing it all down with a cherry slush.

"Just imagine how embarrassing it would be to throw up all over yourself and everyone around you. After your food settles, we'll talk about it."

Her food never "settled".

By the next year, Ellen was sure she would get to ride. After all, she was two years older and a lot taller than the first time she had asked. She even declined the hot dogs, popcorn, cotton candy and cherry slush so she wouldn't have to worry about throwing up all over everyone, but her mother had read in the paper about some kid in some town north of Adington who had been thrown from a ride at a county fair.

"You just can't trust these small-time rides. What do you expect from a bunch of carnies anyway? I bet they don't know a nut from a bolt in their drunken stupors."

Every year had been the same. Ellen begged and her mother refused. The excuses changed but not the outcome. To the adolescents of Adington, the Dragon's Lair became a status symbol. All the cool kids rode it, with bragging rights to the one who rode it the most times in a row without passing out or throwing up. Ellen was sure she was the only junior high student in the entire school who had never ridden it even once. Then one year she got her chance. Her mother decided to stay home and let her go to the fair with some friends. She was in line for the ride, giggling with her friends and surrounded by the coolest kids in the school when she heard her mother's voice.

"Ellen Marie, what do you think you're doing? Get out

of that line this instant. It's a good thing I decided to come down here and check on you. Otherwise, you'd have gone and embarrassed yourself by spewing your lunch all over everybody on the ride."

Ellen heard the snickers behind her back, felt a hundred sets of eyes staring at her and broke out in a cold sweat. Her face was hot. Tears stung her eyes. She followed her mother out of the fair in silence, swallowing her anger until she thought she would be sick.

That was the last year she went to the Monroe County fair. A month later, her father filed for divorce and left Adington. The courts awarded custody to her mother, but three years later, after her father found out that his ex-wife had started to drink excessively, he filed for custody and won. Ellen left Adington, and with the exception of holidays, she hadn't been back, not until she got the call from her aunt Louise that her mother was dying of cirrhosis of the liver and didn't she think she ought to come see her just one last time.

※

"Mom, can I ride it, please? It's totally awesome. Please. I promise I'll clean my room every night and eat all my peas at supper and let Aunt Louise kiss me on the mouth and everything. Please, can I ride it? Pleeeeease."

In a voice that wasn't quite her own, Ellen heard herself saying, "I don't know Evan. You're a little young for that ride. Besides, you just ate. Maybe we should ride some other rides first and come back here after your cotton candy settles."

Evan's bottom lip began to quiver. His shoulders dropped and the enthusiasm and excitement that had been

shining in his eyes all afternoon disappeared. He stood there chewing on his bottom lip, waiting.

She closed her eyes and took a deep breath.

"I'll make a deal with you. You can go on the dragon ride under one condition."

"Anything, Mommy. I promise."

"OK, here it is. You can go on the ride if I can go with you."

Evan took off at a dead run for the Dragon's Lair. He grinned up at his mother as she slid in line behind him.

Contributors

Marian Allen lives in a big house in a little wood, which is not the only difference between Allen and Laura Ingels Wilder. Allen has three novels on electronic disk (alternatively known as "coasters"), and has two novels currently being agented to paper. Wish her luck.

Jeannine Baumgartle writes poetry and fiction. Her work has appeared in publications such as *Green Meadow Press*, *Literally*, and *A Journal for Christians Writing* and recently won a residency for poetry at the Mary Anderson Center for the Arts . She and her husband live in the small town of Crandall with their two children.

Marla Bilbrey the mother of four home schooled children she personally birthed, plus a few that she hasn't seen (but knows live with her) named Ida No, Nota Me, Hee Didit and Leaveme Alone. As an ambitious livestock breeder her prime specimen is her cow that she hoped would be pregnant, but found out it was a male bovine. She lives in New Salisbury, IN. She likes to write on humor, religious and historical topics.

Ginny Fleming doesn't know the meaning of the word "Fear." The pages "F" through "G" are missing from her Funk & Wagnal. Credits include three optioned sitcom scripts, two movie scripts traveling on a slow train around

Hollywood and a novel under consideration. She traces her roots to Milltown (Miller-Perkins) and leaves her heart in Sarasota.

Dirk Griffin Alas — we mourn the late Dirk Griffin. He was so late he almost didn't make this book. If he was any later, we wouldn't have this bio — but we anticipated him. We wrote it anyway. Dirk is survived by unwilling family, a passel of friends, a gaggle of enemies, creditors, and a plethora of nodding acquaintances. Dirk — we hardly knew ye.

Elizabeth J. Gross has won awards for her poetry. She lives in New Salisbury, IN in her dream home; a two-story farmhouse. She receives her living from the river, writing is just a hobby.

T Lee Harris lives in New Albany with a multitude of cats, one Chow-Labrador mix, one goat in a dog-suit, and one humanoid housemate. Publication credits include illustrations and panel-to-panel comic strips in: *The Indiana University Southeast Student, The Huntingburg Herald, Fantaco's Spiderman Chronicles, Fantaco's Fantastic Four Chronicles* and various packages of shareware. T has completed a novel and is at work on the sequel.

Joy Kirchgessner is an illustrator and writer. Her work was recently on tour with the Kentucky National Art and Wildlife Exhibition. She shares her home with her husband, two horses and a very big dog of indeterminate parentage.

Glenda Mills lives with her husband and two children in Floyd County. When she is not busy with homemaking and homeschooling, she writes fiction, nonfiction and poetry. She is presently working on her first fiction novel.

Other Titles in the
Indian Creek Anthology Series:
Indian Creek Anthology
Ghost Writers
Christmas Bizarre
Dragon: Our Tales
Grounds for Suspicion
2000 Tales
Way Out West
Unbridled Lust
There's Something Under the Bedtime Stories
Novel Ingredients
Write of Passage
Off the Rack
Beastly Tales
It's Always Something
Most Wanted
Future Perfect: Tense in Space
Holiday Bizarre
Pair of Normal What?

Visit our web site for excerpts of previous publications
and availability information:

http://southernindianawriters.com
Also by Southern Indiana Writers' Group:
Ghosts: On the Square . . . And Elsewhere . . . .

www.ingramcontent.com/pod-product-compliance
Lightning Source LLC
Chambersburg PA
CBHW060354180626
46817CB00008B/3009